A
Question
of
Destiny

A
Question
of
Destiny

PAMELA F. SERVICE

Atheneum   1986   New York

Library of Congress Cataloging-in-Publication Data

Service, Pamela F.
A question of destiny.

"An Argo book."
SUMMARY: During Dan's father's campaign for
the presidential nomination, he becomes suspicious
that something is very wrong about one of
his father's advisors.
[1. Politics, Practical—Fiction. 2. Mystery and
detective stories] 3. Science Fiction I. Title.
PZ7.S4885Qu 1986 [Fic] 85-21466
ISBN 0-689-31181-8

Published simultaneously in Canada by
Collier Macmillan Canada, Inc.
Text set by Maryland Linotype, Baltimore, Maryland
Printed and bound by
Fairfield Graphics, Fairfield, Pennsylvania
Designed by Marjorie Zaum
First Edition

for Bob
and for Alex, Mark, and
other political kids

A
Question
of
Destiny

Chapter 1

The minute he did it, Dan Stratton wished he hadn't closed the counselor's door quite so hard. He could see her now behind that door, shaking her head and checking off another mark for maladjustment.

But he wasn't maladjusted! These Washington DC teachers were so supersensitive about teaching VIP's kids, they assumed they all had adjustment problems. And now that his dad was running for President, they couldn't believe that somehow he wasn't coming all unglued.

Heck, his dad had been in Congress since before he was born and had been elected to the Senate eight years ago when Dan was in first grade. This just meant more meetings and more press hanging around. Big deal.

The bell blared. Seconds later doors burst open, and the long silent halls flooded with the sound of feet, clattering lockers, and loud mingled voices.

Dan flowed with the tide to his own locker and mechanically twirled the combination lock. Of course, he admitted to himself, he wouldn't claim there was no difference in being the kid of somebody "important." Certainly different things happened to him and his family. But things aren't very special if they're not different to you, no matter how different they are to other people.

On the other hand, the son of Senator Ben Stratton had a lot more expected of him—in grades and behavior. Teachers wouldn't ignore minor infractions for him as they might for other kids, for fear they'd be accused of toadyism. He'd learned that lesson well enough. He supposed that if there was something he really resented, it would be that—people seeing him only as Senator Stratton's son instead of as Dan Stratton, period.

Stuffing in his geometry book, he swung his pack over his shoulder and trudged back down the crowded hall. The counselor was just coming out of her door. Quickly Dan studied the mural on the opposite wall.

He tried as well to ignore most of the kids around him. He might not be any different since his dad had announced for President two weeks ago, but people were certainly treating him differently. He'd never had many close friends, but now some kids were attaching themselves like leeches, boasting no doubt that a "real good friend" of theirs might live in the White House next year. Most, however, avoided him awkwardly, as though a close relative of his had died and they didn't know what to say.

He looked up to see one of the "good buddy" types bearing down on him. He glanced around; nowhere to hide.

"Danny boy," the boy said slapping him on the shoulder, "how'd you do on that social studies test? Bet you knocked their socks off! I told the kids you would."

"Oh, well, Joe, I got by okay." He smiled weakly, thinking he'd like to trap this guy in a locker and forget the combination. Just because his dad was in politics, why should he know all about Roosevelt's Supreme Court? Joe's father was a broker, so could Joe automatically pass a test on grain futures and international conglomerates?

He slipped his shoulder out of the other's hearty grip. "Got to go, Joe, or I'll miss my bus. Talk to you tomorrow." Unless I see you first, he added to himself.

In the main foyer, he stopped, pulled the knitted cap from his pocket and jammed it down over his tousled sandy-colored hair. Outside the high glass arches, an early snow fell in a silent white curtain. On gusts of cold, it swirled in through the constantly opening doors. He just wished it had come on a weekend, not uselessly in the middle of the week when there was school in the day and homework at night.

Whiteness gusted over the stone steps as he and

the others hurried down them toward the bus stops. He stuck his hands into his pockets, not bothering with mittens. Head down against the snow, he brushed past a larger boy who turned and shouted after him. "What, don't Strattons travel by horse and buggy?"

Dan didn't have to turn to see who it was. Big Bruce, son of the fellow his dad called the most acid-tongued columnist in town. Acidity, he guessed, ran in the family.

Dan ignored him, as he knew you're supposed to with hecklers. It generally made them mad but shut them up. Only it didn't this time.

The stocky boy hurried ahead of him and slammed a hand against his chest. "Now, important person, aren't you going to give us a speech about space versus earth? How does it go, 'using man's resources on man, not machines'?"

"What's the point?" Dan said, trying to appear more calm than he was. He pushed the hand aside and shoved past. "You're too pigheaded to understand it."

Cringing inwardly, he hurried on. That had not been smart. He was tall for his fourteen years, but Bruce was built like an ox. Still, Bruce didn't seem to fight, not with the Candidate's kid, anyway. At the moment, that was one spin-off Dan was happy to accept.

He joined the clump of bundled-up kids waiting for his bus. A few feet ahead of him he picked out the short, plumpish figure of Carla Brenner. Her hood was back, and snow lay in large flakes on her wavy black hair. She was one of his few real friends since Dick Lenox had moved away. And she treated him like a friend, not something to be fawned over or be in awe of.

Maybe that was because her own dad had won a Nobel Prize when they'd lived in some small town. They'd become instant celebrities, and she'd learned just how phony that all was. Of course, her folks were divorced now, and her father lived in Australia or someplace. But her mother was a physicist too, and important scientists were always hanging around. Carla was refreshingly unimpressed.

The bus was filling up as Dan dropped into an empty seat beside Carla and started brushing snow-flakes from his jacket.

"I heard Big Mouth Bruce's stupid comments," she said unzipping her jacket. "One thing your dad's announcement's done is make the space issue a real hot item around here. We talked about it in social studies today. Afterwards, Susan Guthrie came up and asked me if your dad let you see space movies or play video games."

"And you told her I was locked in my room after school with nothing but shelves of Shakespeare and Mark Twain for company."

"No, you jerk, I told her the truth; that you have every Star Trek episode practically memorized and play a pretty mean game of Space Pirates."

"Thanks. And you could have mentioned my Chewbacca lunchbox in third grade."

It was getting steamy in the crowded bus. Dan unzipped his jacket. "Why can't those turkeys see the difference? All that is far future and fantasy stuff. You know, 'long, long ago in a galaxy far away.' It's got nothing to do with the space program. That's just dull technicians crammed into orbiting tin cans that'd make Scotty laugh himself silly. Even the moon base is just a collection of dumb experiments visited by bundled-up repairmen. Bah! Darth Vader wouldn't bother invading us."

The kids on the seats around them had stopped jabbering and were listening. He should shut up, but the anger he'd held back wanted out. And Carla was always a willing debater.

"Sure, I know it isn't space opera stuff yet," she said, "but we have to start somewhere. Besides, what about all those spin-off things—Teflon and all those medical discoveries?"

"Come on, I'm not saying we shouldn't ever go into space. And sure it's got to be done one step at a time. But right now we've got too many other things to do down here. We could've lived without Teflon, and if a little of the money spent on space had been given *directly* to medical research we'd have a lot more medical discoveries by now. And what about all those people starving in Africa, or the ones right here in Washington who don't even have heat in their houses?"

8

Dan scowled out the bus window at the gray buildings sliding by behind ragged drapes of snow. That ghetto he'd worked in with the youth group, it was out there, with its flimsy walls and broken windows. Maybe those people were no more needy than the spindly African children on the TV news, but their hurt was something he had touched. Guilt jabbed him. He shouldn't unload on Carla. She knew a lot more about poverty than he did.

He smiled at her sheepishly. "Hey, sorry. I didn't mean to speechify."

She smiled back, dark eyes glinting in a dusky face. "That's okay. I just argue to keep you in form."

The bus rumbled on through the snowy streets. Carla leaned back and looked out the window. She liked Dan. He tended to lecture when he got worked up about something, but he was right about people needing help. She'd seen that on the reservation when her mother had fallen back on her family after the divorce. People were poor there, awfully poor, and hadn't much hope. After a couple years, her mother had broken away again, using her hard-earned degree to scrape by in the white man's world and raise her children. But all those others were trapped in poverty. It wasn't right.

She sighed, then looked at Dan. A serious frown still cramped his face. She smiled playfully. "Would you get really mad if I said you sound just like your dad? We heard him on TV last night. Even my mom, with her physics and all, says she thinks he's right."

"No, I'm not mad! And better stop thinking I would be or you'll be just like those busybody counselors!"

"Oh, now you are mad."

He growled in mock fury. "You're hopeless! Let's talk about something fun like Latin verbs."

Several stops past Carla's, the bus let Dan off. A yellow blaze on the winter-bleak streets, it rumbled off leaving him alone in the silence. The snow wasn't very cold, but it was wet. Soft flakes fell in a steady curtain that muffled the sounds of the city.

Hands thrust into his pockets, he walked up the wide street. The snow crunched under his feet as he kicked arches of white through the air ahead of him. Lights glowed from windows of colonial style houses, and wreaths bedecked their doors. It seemed like walking by a row of giant Christmas cards.

What he'd told Carla was true, he mused as he trudged along. He really did agree with his dad. No matter what the counselors thought, he didn't resent him. He liked him and respected him, and really believed he was right. He did wish he had more time with him, and this Presidential thing wasn't going to help. But he was proud to be Ben Stratton's son—he just wanted to be something else besides.

He kicked a hard lump of snow that had been plowed onto the curb. With a dull thunk, it rolled into the street. What he wanted didn't have to be anything splashy. He definitely didn't need to "make a name for himself." He'd seen enough of that. But he did want to do something important on his own, so that if people kept calling him Ben Stratton's son, he at least would know he was something more.

Of course, he still wasn't exactly sure what it was that he wanted to do. But it certainly wasn't politics. Bean suppers and hand-shaking; long weary meetings and people you didn't even know calling you nasty names. In politics, colleagues could be your friend one minute and stab you in the back the next. No thanks. It was a hard, demanding business with little privacy and less thanks. He'd find something else.

Scooping up a handful of snow, he packed it into a ball and hurled it at the stone lion guarding the gate of a neighbor's home. It splattered satisfyingly over the arrogant face. Archaeology was his current leaning. The people you dealt with there were good and dead, but the mysteries and discoveries were just as worthwhile as any political cause. Yes, if he needed a hero besides his dad, he'd probably take Indiana Jones —without the snakes.

A cluster of cars was parked in front of his house, and the snow on the front path looked freshly trampled down. Another meeting. Slipping in the front door, he dropped his backpack at the foot of the stairs and headed for the kitchen. Voices rose and fell in the front room.

His mom had left a note on the refrigerator. She was giving a speech somewhere. The apple pie was for dinner, but he could have the remains of the blueberry one. Opening the refrigerator he scrutinized the pie. Not enough left to bother with a plate. Dropping a fork onto the pie tin, he poured himself a glass of milk and, hands full, walked into the front room.

Flopping down on the couch, he dug into the pie. Half a dozen people were clustered at the other end of the room by the French windows. Among them sat Ben Stratton, junior senator from Indiana, looking even more rumpled and disheveled than the cartoonists usually showed him. No matter how well-fitting the suit, Dan mused, it wrinkled the instant his dad put it on. And his hair never stayed combed. Not, Dan admitted, that he was much better. His mother claimed sloppiness must be hereditary.

The group was talking about possible rivals for the nomination. For a while Dan munched his pie and listened. There was that old warhorse, Babcock, who hadn't declared yet, but everyone expected to; and there was Governor LaSalle of Louisiana. He was handsome as a soaps star and already running hard. Helene Kulani, congresswoman from Hawaii, was the strongest liberal contender, while Oregon's Senator Vonderman seemed to be the standard bearer for the conservative wing. These were the major rivals in their own party, but on the other side the choice was clear. Two-term President Wainwright could not succeed himself and was backing his Vice-President, Fred Hambly.

Dan had heard all of the general stuff before

and wasn't much interested in details of polls and endorsements. Most of the people here were getting to be as familiar about the place as furniture. Sam Lederman, the campaign manager, had been with his dad only a year, but Roger McKenzie was a friend from college, and David Greer had been with them since the first senate campaign. Greer, with his cold formality, his prematurely gray hair, and his perpetual dark glasses operated a computer system that was supposedly the heart of the campaign. But Dan had never cared for him.

Bored, Dan picked up the new *National Geographic* from the coffee table. Blue tattoed people on some island, colonies of sponges, a weird-looking species of bird, and finally something interesting—another new archeological site near Pompeii. Super pictures of bodies made out of compressed ash. That's what he'd like to do, all right, discover a site like that, or at least be the guy with the whiskbroom exposing an ancient mosaic. They were revealing a mystery, showing something totally new about people's lives. That was worth doing.

When he'd finished the article, Dan flipped the magazine back onto the table. Across the room David Greer was intoning, "Not all the aerospace workers are leaning to LaSalle. The latest poll shows him perceived as weak on the issue. Among that group there's been a seven point six percent shift to Vonderman in the last month."

"So the longer they both stay in the race, the better for us," McKenzie said.

"Only on that one issue," Greer replied in his dry, slightly accented voice. "Now on the environmental question . . ."

Swigging down the last of his milk, Dan left the room. He grabbed his pack and trudged upstairs. Homework time. Boring, but not as boring as campaign talk.

Kicking open the door of his room, he pulled a book from his pack and flopped down on the bed. With all the exciting things to read in this world, how could they be stuck with Dickens? Doggedly he plowed through another chapter, then almost with relief he turned to his desk and geometry. Laying the textbook out on his desk, he rummaged again through the pack for his calculator. He practically tore the seams apart but couldn't find it.

Blast! He must have left it in his locker. There was no way, though, that he was going to do all that math longhand. They were allowed to use calculators, and he had every intention of doing so.

He'd go downstairs for his dad's. It was probably in his study. But once downstairs, Dan realized the meeting had adjourned to the study, and he hated barging in. He stopped in the middle of the living room wondering where his mother kept the calculator she used for shopping. Probably had it with her.

As he stood frowning, his eye fell on an end

table. There, like the answer to a magic wish, lay a calculator. It was David Greer's; he recognized it, though he'd seldom seen Greer without it in his hand.

It was an interesting-looking model. He reached to pick it up and was surprised at the feel. The metal casing felt oddly liquid and heavy, though it actually didn't seem to weigh more than usual. The shape was a little different from the average pocket model, and it had an unusually large blank space above the screen.

He dropped down into a chair and examined his find. The equations he ran through came out all right, but there were a few extra keys he couldn't find the purpose for. No matter what he did with them they didn't seem to affect the readout.

He turned the thing over, poking and examining everything. The surface really felt weird, but there were no more controls, only a decorative flange along the side. He pressed this and was about to move on when a second glowing screen appeared above the first. The surface there had seemed perfectly smooth and blank before.

He tried pressing keys again. Nothing happened on the second screen until he also pressed one of the mystery keys. Then, while he worked the regular keys, figures flashed on the top screen. But these weren't numerals or normal letters. They were very strange signs. He'd never seen anything like them.

He kept pressing keys, and symbols appeared,

the same ones occasionally repeating. He worked at it again and again until some of the signs were becoming familiar. But he had no idea what they meant.

A hand gripped his shoulder. "Don't meddle with my things, Danny." Greer's voice was sharp and cold.

Startled, Dan gripped the calculator, and it popped out of his hand like a wet bar of soap. Before he could retrieve it from the rug, Greer scooped it up.

"Fortunately for you, the material is tough," the man snapped. Dan couldn't see behind the reflective dark glasses, but he imagined the look was piercing.

"I'm sorry—"

"Good. Don't do it again—ever." The small, neatly dressed man turned abruptly and stalked back to the study.

In the split second the calculator had lain on the rug, Dan had seen that in slipping from his hand the extra screen had been turned off. He hoped Greer hadn't noticed that he'd discovered it. He felt that would compound his transgression.

Dan was surprised to find he was actually shaking. That supercilious jerk made his skin crawl. He got up and slowly walked upstairs. At his desk, he resolutely opened the geometry book only to stare blankly at its pages.

Taking up a pencil, he slowly began drawing the symbols he'd seen. He remembered a number of them. Some he knew weren't quite right, but the feeling was there. Oddly angular.

Finally he leaned back and studied what he had

done. The symbols certainly were strange—strange in that they struck no familiar cords. He'd seen nothing quite like them. They couldn't be mathematical symbols, he was familiar with most of those. They weren't shorthand, and didn't look like Arabic or Hebrew. They certainly weren't Chinese or Japanese.

What about Russian? He reached to a bookshelf and pulled out a multi-language dictionary. Plunking it open on his desk, he began flipping through for the Russian. Suddenly he stopped cold. Russian. He remembered Greer's faint trace of accent. Could he be . . . ?

No, that was too absurd. Hurriedly he turned to the first page of the Russian section. The letters weren't all that odd. Nothing like these symbols.

The knots inside him loosened. But the seed was sown. This still might be some sort of foreign language or code. Greer was certainly protective of that calculator. And he was an awfully private guy, secretive even. Suppose he . . .

Dan grabbed at his mind, trying to shake some sense into it. Greer had been with his dad for years. He could hardly be a foreign spy! Get on with the geometry, he told himself. It'll take twice as long without a calculator.

A while later, his mother called him to dinner. He was relieved to see that the others, particularly David Greer, had gone.

Chapter 2

At school the next day, the strange symbols swam vaguely in the back of Dan's mind. He doodled them on the edge of his papers. But he thought he had the thing in perspective now. The fear he'd felt at the suggestion of Russian agents still scratched at him. But today he saw the whole thing as a puzzle, a mystery to be solved—not necessarily sinister, but possibly important.

After school, he decided to go to the public library and look up more scripts. The puzzle might not be worthy of Sherlock Holmes, but it was his own personal challenge. He'd find out Greer's secret, petty though it probably was.

Slipping away from both fawners and hecklers, he passed up the school buses and walked to the nearest city bus stop. To his surprise, Carla was waiting there too, dark hair framed in the white fur hood. The sky was gray and heavy with pending snow, and the air was bitingly cold.

Carla looked up. Seeing Dan approaching broke her gloomy mood. She'd been thinking of the dinky house where she, her brother, sister and cousins would be crammed together for the next who-knows-how-many months. She wished her mother hadn't taken that job, good pay or not.

"You going to the library, too?" Dan asked as he stopped beside her.

"No, I'm staying with some cousins for a while. They're not on the school bus routes. My mom's going off to Nevada to work on some research project."

"Oh? Sounds exciting. What's the project about?"

"Don't know. It's so top secret she can't tell us much about it. Some jerk called Dr. Svengard is running it. I've met him. He's a real creep, but the pay's good."

"Looks like my bus," Dan said as a city bus lumbered around a corner and squeaked to a stop in a cloud of exhaust.

Quickly Carla tore off a corner from a notebook page and scribbled down her new phone number. "Call me sometime and give me a break from squalling kids and barking dogs. I may go mad there."

Grabbing the paper, Dan hopped onto the bus. It jerked forward, flopping him into a seat as he tried to cram the phone number into his wallet.

Carla was a fun person, he thought. He wondered if he should tell her about his current project. No, not 'til he had something to tell her. Then maybe they could look the mystery over together.

Dan's search at the library led him through a tangle of languages, ancient and modern, some of which he'd never known existed. But none contained the symbols he sought. Working in the large, dauntingly quiet reference room, he looked at Tibetan, Mongolian, and Lao; and at cuneiform, runic and Egyptian hieroglyphics. After these and half a dozen others, he skimmed several books on code. Nothing.

The mystery was getting more and more frustrating. He wished, as he had many times before, that Dick Lenox's father had been reelected to Congress last time. Dick had liked mysteries, too. Together they'd played "the Hardy Boys" solving various absurd mysteries of their own creation. And sometimes Dan played Dr. Watson to Dick's Sherlock Holmes. Dick was the taller and more Holmesian of the two.

Maybe he'd write Dick after dinner. On second thought, he'd better wait. He didn't really know what he had, and the thought made him uneasy. He'd better hold off mentioning it to Carla, too. Anyway, he'd run into a dead end here. A glance up at the library's ancient clock told him he'd have to hurry home.

His mother met him at their door. Short, plump and always neat, Emma Stratton was a contrast to her rumpled, gangly husband. Her smile at Dan was taut with worry and relief.

"Where were you? I was beginning to get worried."

"Sorry. I should have phoned. I stopped at the library to do some research."

"Well, do call next time. Your father's going to be assigned some secret service people soon, and they're already lecturing us about how candidates need to keep close track of where their children are."

"Hey, they're not going to stick me with a body-guard, are they?"

"Not if you're a good little boy," she teased.

"Bleah!"

The idea of having a secret service babysitter following him around was bloodcurdling. Certain of his schoolmates would have fun with that. Then another thought struck him. If his dad actually got elected, they might try to make him go to a private school. He'd certainly fight that one. Better the pains he knew than the snobs he didn't. The whole thing almost took his appetite away—almost.

After second helpings were disposed of and the dinner dishes cleared away, Dan spread his geography homework over the dining room table. He was supposed to draw boundaries, cities and rivers of various African countries, countries whose names seemed to change with every map and globe. He wished they'd make a choice and stick with it.

From the kitchen behind him came the clatter of washing dishes and the lingering and no longer enticing smell of pork chops. Voices drifted through the half-opened door to the study. His dad was in there with Lederman and McKenzie. The Hoosier drawls of Stratton and McKenzie were cut by the other's sharp New York twang.

Minutes passed. The men's conversation washed in and out of Dan's hearing as he concentrated on the rivers of Africa. The topics had changed several times when McKenzie said, "Now this is something we'd better take care of before we get any further into the campaign. We've been checking on the backgrounds of all our top aides, present and contemplated. If there are skeletons in any closets, we need to know now— before something can be turned into an issue."

"So what have you cloak and dagger boys come up with?"

"Here are dossiers on everyone we've checked so far," Lederman said to the sound of shuffling paper. "Myers had some questionable stock dealings, insider's profits maybe, but that was years ago. He's been more careful since. Margaret White is as clean as her name. Wrenn was expelled for cheating in college but got reinstated."

More shuffling. McKenzie's voice. "Now this is David Greer's file." Instantly Dan lost all interest in the course of the Limpopo River. "Basically it seems all right, but there are a few gaps. We have his army records from when he served in one of those middle eastern things. That's where he supposedly met the grenade that injured his eyes. But I couldn't find any army medical records—no mention of treatment there or in the States. And he doesn't seem to be getting any disability payments."

"Let me see that," the Senator said.

"Of course, records can get lost," McKenzie continued. "So I attacked it from the other end. I know the fellow who was in charge of that particular skirmish, slightly anyway, so I called him to ask about Greer, and he had no recollection of him. He was certain Greer had never served under him, although the records say that he had."

"Roger," Stratton said with exasperation. "I know David isn't your favorite person. I suppose none of us has ever warmed to him. But he's been with us eight years now. He's as loyal as a dog, if not as friendly. With this checkup, I'm not concerned about misplaced records or memories, but with gross misconduct. Now, unless you've got something big on our people, let's look at our vice-presidential choices. We certainly don't want any nasty surprises there."

Dan tried to absorb himself in Africa again, but it wasn't easy. Finally finishing all the required lines, he stacked up his books and papers, hassled his mother for a bowl of ice cream, and went upstairs to bed.

He lay there a long while after finishing the ice cream. Sleep bounced off him like an acrobat off a trampoline. A detective in a mystery he'd read once had said, "One and one are simple numbers by themselves, but together they make two." A stupid line—but true.

Still, fantasy aside, he was no detective. He

should end this investigation right now. There was, however, one thing he wanted to do first, look at that file on David Greer. Holmes would at least have Watson do that.

He sat up in bed, leaning against the cool wooden headboard. After a while he heard voices in the downstairs hall. The front door opened and closed, two cars drove away in the night. Soon afterwards his parents came upstairs. The bathroom door closed several times, the toilet flushed, water ran. Finally the house settled down to its own quiet creakings.

Wtih heart thumping, Dan slipped out of bed and threw on a bathrobe. He dropped his bedside flashlight into a pocket and opened the door a crack. The hall was dark. No light showed under his parents' door. The only noise was the ponderous ticking of the hall clock downstairs.

He slipped out the door, closing it softly behind him. Bare feet padded over carpet to the top of the stairs. Cautiously he descended, stepping carefully over the creaking fifth stair. But he forgot the seventh.

It creaked explosively. He froze, every muscle taut as a spring. Seconds passed, a minute. Nothing.

Breathing again, he continued to the bottom and sped like a ghost through the house until he came to his father's study. Once safe inside, he switched on the flashlight.

He flashed the beam around the room. He wasn't sure where those reports would be filed. Under "P" for personnel? "S" for staff?

His light crisscrossed again halting on the table. He needn't bother with cabinets. The files were still out. His father was never in a hurry to be orderly.

After thumbing through a dozen or so manila folders, he pulled out one marked "D. Greer," and opened it. The game is afoot, he quoted to himself as he flipped through the pages. But the information proved far from earthshaking. He learned where Greer was born and grew up (Indianapolis). What schools he attended and his grades (depressingly good). His courses in college. His birthmarks (none), and allergies (ragweed). Nothing suspicious there. His army record was there minus a medical addendum as McKenzie had said. And there was other material, all equally bland.

Dan closed the folder, unsure whether he should be satisfied or disappointed. He wasn't even sure what he had been looking for. There'd hardly be an entry about Greer attending KGB school in Moscow. The report didn't say if his parents were some sort of immigrants to explain the accent, but then it didn't say they weren't.

Still, to be thorough, he should have copies of all of this. Then maybe he could put this whole questionable investigation on hold.

His dad's copying machine stood bulkily in the corner. He looked at it doubtfully. It was quieter than most copiers, but the house itself was awfully quiet just now. Still, he might not get another chance. These files might go to another office.

Before he could have third and fourth thoughts, he walked to the machine, lifted the top, slid in the first page and pressed the button. A whir awoke, and an eerie green light moved along the bottom of the paper.

He waited breathlessly for a minute, but nothing stirred in the rest of the house. He copied the next sheet and the next. He'd slipped into a mechanical routine when he heard a sound in the dining room.

Quickly he flung himself over the machine to hide the light and sound. Slippers padded over the dining room floor. They turned into the kitchen. His dad was after a midnight snack.

He heard the refrigerator door open. Quietly Dan picked up the file and his copies and crouched down beside a much-too-narrow cabinet. It seemed hours before the footsteps left the kitchen. They crossed the dining room, then paused outside the study door. The doorknob shifted as a hand was placed upon it.

The faint sound repeated as the hand withdrew. Sleep had won out over work. Dan breathed a prayer of thanks.

Minutes passed before he dared stand up and make the last hurried copies. Then carefully replacing the originals in the right order, he eased the file back into its proper place in the pile. Tucking the rolled copies into a bathrobe pocket, Dan swiftly retraced his steps, avoiding both the fifth and seventh stairs.

Back in his room again, he leaned against the

closed door until he stopped shaking. Then he slid the copies under his mattress. Thinking better of it, he retrieved them and pulling an atlas from a shelf, filed them under Zaire. Then he climbed into bed and let his nerves gradually unwind.

This whole thing was ludicrous. What if his dad had come in and found him crouching like a burglar beside the file cabinet? Even Dr. Watson didn't get himself into scrapes like that. And what would he do with all these puzzle pieces anyway?

Never mind. It was foolish. But it could just possibly be important. And it was something he was doing on his own. Big deal, he told himself. But one part of his drowsing mind told him it just might be.

Chapter 3

The political year continued. To the surprise of poll-sters, Ben Stratton did well in some of the early primaries. After weeks of campaigning in snow-clogged New Hampshire, he won that primary, and shortly afterwards he came in a strong second in the more congenial climate of Georgia. The media now paid him, and his family, more attention. Stratton was hardly a front-runner, but his campaign theme, "the human race not the space race," was drawing notice and he was treated as less of a joke. Press people even pinned Dan down a few times, but he managed to slip away after a few "typical American boy" type remarks.

In his own particular campaign, Dan was making less progress. He couldn't do much to check out his information. It took pull to call up people at the Pentagon, and no one took a fourteen year old seriously. He didn't even have enough solid suspicions to voice them to his father or to Roger McKenzie. The only thing he could do, he decided, was to keep an eye on David Greer, watching for any sign of campaign sabotage or suspicious activity. That was one thing Dr. Watson was always good at—watching the suspects.

This meant closely following every aspect of the campaign, because it became clear that Greer's campaign computer was central to everything. Not only did it contain statistics and information on thousands of individuals, it held facts on the economy and defense that were easily obtainable only by insiders in the United States Senate.

Suppose, Dan worried, Greer's aim wasn't to destroy Ben Stratton but to use him? Suppose the whole thing was only an elaborate scheme for channeling information to his mysterious bosses?

And suppose, Dan also told himself, he was being a silly kid letting his imagination run on practically no facts! Still, he kept working for the campaign. He would have anyway; he wanted his dad to win. But it wouldn't hurt to keep a cautious eye open as well.

Often, after school, he dropped by the downtown "Stratton for President" headquarters to help address envelopes, make phone calls or run errands. The place had once been a discount shoe store, but was now festooned with flags and bunting, and its walls and picture windows were plastered with posters. Dan was used to seeing giant-sized pictures of his dad. But he found the huge family portraits, with himself grinning at him from all directions, rather unnerving. The giant glower of Blimbo the family cat, shown firmly clamped in his mother's lap, was just plain weird.

While making himself useful around headquarters, Dan also asked what he hoped were discreet questions. Gradually he began building up a picture of David Greer. Nobody seemed to know him very well. He was an efficient and tireless worker, but personally cold and distant. He never mentioned any family and apparently had no girl friends. The perfect spy personality, Dan thought, but also one that was hard to pin anything on.

His father, pleased with Dan's apparent new interest, commented on it one rainy April afternoon when, for a few rare moments, they were alone together in a headquarters backroom.

"So, you think maybe politics isn't such a bad field after all?"

Dan blushed, hoping it wouldn't show in the grayish light. "Oh, it's okay—make a good anthropological study for someone."

His father chuckled. "So that's why you're always asking questions. Anthropological research?"

"Being an anthropologist wouldn't be so bad,

would it?" Dan replied with diversionary defensiveness.

"Oh no. But as a reliable living, it's almost as bad as politics."

Dan didn't reply. At least he'd turned attention from his real motives. He was getting good at these political skills—and didn't like it.

Just then McKenzie and speechwriter Bill Blair bustled into the room. "There you are, Ben," McKenzie said. "Wainwright's speech this morning was a good sign, don't you think?"

"How so?"

"Spending that much time defending their space policy means he sees you as a serious threat. The media'll pick up on that."

Blair plunked his fat body down in a folding chair and thumbed through a sheaf of notes. "He had a line you can use, too. 'This coming election poses a question of destiny for America and mankind.' You can say, right, it does, and the question is if our destiny is to continue ignoring the needy while we build expensive toys in dead space. Something like that."

Dan joined a group of college students who had deferentially slipped into the room and spread their mailing project over one table. As the candidate and advisors talked, Dan watched the girl opposite him, her eyes widening with excitement. Here was Her Candidate making Important Decisions right before her eyes.

Dan shrugged and began sticking on address labels. He figured that the excitingness of something must depend on its extraordinariness. He'd heard this girl mention her mother singing in opera. Now that was exciting! But a bunch of adults sitting around talking politics—that was dullness personified.

Eventually the school year drew to an end. Dan asked Carla to the end-of-semester dance. No romantic intentions, but she was a good companion. And by taking her, he was safe from all those other girls who'd been stalking him since it looked as if he could become the President's son.

Carla's mother, he learned, was still off doing secret scientific work in Nevada while Carla and her little brother and sister remained jammed in their cousins' house. He'd talked with her on the phone and even gone with her to a few movies to keep up her spirits.

This summer she planned to keep from going crazy by enrolling in a Smithsonian program on the culture of Southwestern American Indians. Whereas her mother, in fighting for her physics degree, had sought to escape her Indian heritage, Carla had accepted and enjoyed it. Dan envied her. She had something that was special to her, something to hold onto inside.

With the close of school, the Strattons officially went back home to Indiana. Senator Stratton, of course, commuted regularly between Washington and his constituency. But Dan and his mother usually stayed in the Washington house during the school year and returned during the summer to the old farmhouse east of Bloomington.

Dan was glad. Washington was a lousy place to spend the summer: hot, muggy and crowded with tourists. And Bloomington was his real home. He realized that again, as he did every time, when he stepped into the cool high-ceilinged parlor and breathed in the familiar, slightly musty smell of the place.

Of course, this wasn't a working farm anymore. Just the old Victorian house and a few acres of grass and woods. The only livestock were squirrels, a continuous supply of cats in the saggy barn, and several stolid ducks, which paddled around the scummy pond.

But Dan loved it, a little oasis of freedom. He hadn't been altogether happy when his father had finally decided to move the family to Washington. And though he hadn't gone to school with them since the fourth grade, Dan still had a few friends here he kept in touch with. He was almost afraid to ask them over now, though he found it hard to believe that they'd be struck with son-of-possible-President awe. Surely they'd all gone through too much messing around together for that.

The whole Stratton family, however, didn't stay at the farmhouse long. And while they did, the usual quiet of the place was trampled by reporters looking for "color" and "human interest." After a few days his parents went off campaigning.

Dan had already gone on some campaign trips with them, even taking a few days off school for a swing through the Midwest before the May primaries. The endless succession of rallies and fund-raising dinners had been so tiring and boring that he'd almost lost track of which town or state they were in. He'd felt like a store mannequin, dressed in clean clothes and set smiling on platforms and head tables.

Now his parents were in California, going all out for that key primary. Dan was just as glad to be staying with his aunt in the quiet old house. There'd be activity aplenty when he rejoined his parents for the Convention.

One evening, he and his aunt were sitting on the sagging front porch finishing a pizza and Coke supper. She worked in a law office in town and didn't much like to cook when she got home. That was fine with Dan. To him pizza was the ultimate meal.

The air was warm and so humid Dan felt he could reach out and squeeze drops from it. But it had an antique gentleness about it, soft and sweet with the fragrance of honeysuckle. Insects chirped rythmically in the grass, and fireflies glimmered tentatively among the bushes and dark places under the trees. As the twilight deepened, they became bolder; dancing and twinkling over the lawn and up the dark shapes of trees like random fairy lights.

His aunt was talking about her brother's campaign, in which she took great pride.

"Did you hear the latest thing on the news about Vonderman?"

"No." Dan caught a sagging festoon of cheese with a finger and coiled it back on his slice of pizza. Until recently, he'd seldom listened to the news voluntarily, and in the last few days he'd enjoyed slipping back into his old oblivious ways.

"One of his top aides is accused of taking bribes from some Latin American dictator. It's caused quite a stink, and it's bound to hurt Vonderman in California. Did you hear that Governor Morales has finally come out for your dad there?"

Dan nodded, suddenly tense.

"Well that gives him a really good chance, as long as Kulani doesn't run off with too many minority votes. I like her all right, but she's a spoiler. No chance of winning, just taking votes from Ben. But just think! Barring some sort of disaster, like Vonderman's, you could be sipping Coke on the White House porch next summer!"

Dan was silent, riveted with fear and guilt. There could be a time bomb in their own camp, and he was sitting back doing nothing. But now that he was back in Indiana, there was one thing he could do.

"Aunt Laura, I'm going to get up early and spend the whole day in town tomorrow. There are a lot of things I want to do and places to go. You know, just a day by myself."

"Sure, I know, Danny. A lot of old haunts need visiting. If you're living in the White House next year, you might not get another chance."

He gritted his teeth over the easy lies. "Sure, that's it, I guess."

Next morning he gathered up some savings and bicycled into town. There were few people or cars about yet. Bloomington, a college town, took on a lazy air in the summer, with most of the students away.

He glided smoothly down the wide tree-lined street along the south edge of campus. The early morning sun sparkled in the leaves and gilded the stone of the ivy-twined buildings. The air was still fresh but held the promise of another muggy day.

He swung through the town square. The old domed courthouse sat smugly among its cooing pigeons, stone monuments and mounted cannon. Dan liked the building. It was more human than the cold white temples that glimmered around Washington, the ones that frowned down on mere mortals, daring them to have business there.

At last he pulled into the Greyhound station and chained his bike to the rack. He bought a ticket for Indianapolis and sat for ten nervous minutes in the waiting room, hoping that no one would come in who recognized him. No one did.

When the bus arrived, he took a window seat in the rear and spent the hour and a half trip watching the landscape slowly change from rough wooded hills of southern Indiana to the flat glaciated plains of the corn belt.

The sun-gleaming towers of Indianapolis came into sight, looking at a distance like the beckoning city of Oz. The illusion, he knew, would be ruined soon enough. His dad had once, very much in private, called it "a city with no excuse for itself other than habit." Dan agreed. A nowhere sort of place. Appropriate for David Greer to have grown up in.

Once outside the Indianapolis station, he considered taking a city bus. But he didn't know the routes. Besides, whenever Holmes and Watson went investigating, they took a hansom cab. He flagged down a taxi, the next best thing, and gave the driver the address of Greer's boyhood home he'd found in the copied file.

The taxi headed north, into neighborhoods that had clearly seen more prosperous days. It let him off on the wrong block, but Dan wasn't feeling pushy.

The sky, which had been so clear and sunny earlier, had clouded over. Soot-gray clouds piled against an ash-gray backdrop. A damp wind scuttled bits of paper along the street. Tornado weather, he thought uneasily, and hurriedly walked up the block.

It was not a tidy neighborhood, but the houses had a shabby grandeur and had not yet fallen into slums. Weeds shared the gutters with beer cans and broken glass. But a couple of small children were Big Wheeling happily along the sidewalk.

Dan kept his eyes on the house numbers, some faded or broken off altogether. There was the one he wanted. A squat yellow bungalow, it in no way stood out from its neighbors. He felt a tinge of disappointment. He didn't know what he'd expected. Not neon signs, but something more impressive at the end of his journey. Slowly he walked up the front path. The pavement was cracked, and on either side, rosebushes were losing out to weeds.

On the front porch he hesitated, his stomach tightening. He'd knocked on strangers' doors often enough campaigning for his dad. But then he'd had a handful of literature—and he'd believed in what he was doing. Now . . . ?

He knocked. Nothing. He'd never considered that there might be no one at home. He knocked again, harder.

Footsteps in the hall, and the door opened. A harried-looking woman in a soiled dress stood staring at him. In seconds she was joined by a diapered toddler who clung to her knees and looked up at Dan with thumb in mouth and nose running.

"Yes?" the woman said irritably.

"Oh, yes, sorry. I wonder if you could help me? I'm doing some genealogical research, and I believe some relatives of mine, a family named Greer, lived here about fifteen years ago. I was wondering if you knew anything about them or where they might have gone?"

"Don't know nothing about nobody named

Greer." She yanked the thumb out of the child's mouth. It squalled and jammed the thumb back in. "But we just come here last year. Try the neighbors." She shut the door.

Dejected, Dan walked back to the sidewalk. He'd done better pushing campaign literature. But maybe he should try a neighbor. He just hoped some had been around a bit longer.

He scanned the nearby houses. Observe, Watson, he told himself. Most looked fairly neglected. But the three story frame house on the opposite corner had a different air about it. The garden was tended, and although it could use a coat of paint, the wrought iron fence was intact and still held its swinging gate. White lace curains hung at all the windows.

Resolutely he walked to the door and knocked on the panel of beveled glass. Then seeing the old-fashioned bell, he twisted that for good measure. It rang like a musical cricket. After a moment the door opened several inches and was caught by a chain. A white-haired lady looked out.

"Excuse me, ma'am, but I'm doing some geneological research. Some relatives of mine named Greer lived in the yellow house across the street about fifteen years ago. I'm trying to find out something about them and where they might be now. Can you help?"

"Oh my, young man, let me think." She reached up and unlatched the chain. "Sorry to be so un-friendly, but you can't be too careful these days."

"Yes, I know."

"Well now, what did you say the name was . . . Greer?"

"Yes, ma'am, and the one I'm particularly interested in was the son, David Greer. He should be in his late thirties now."

"Well, the people who live there now, they're new. Don't know much about them. And the ones they bought from were just speculators and hardly lived there at all. Before that there was a young couple named . . . now what was it? Hartley, I believe. Yes, Beth and Joe Hartley. Nice young people. He worked in insurance or some such, and she stayed home with the sweetest little baby. But they moved away, don't remember where now. But it wasn't them you was needing to know about, was it?"

"No, ma'am, the Greers."

"Well, I don't see how Greers could fit in, because the Hartleys bought the house from old Mrs. Bridgefield herself, and she'd lived there some forty years before that. Her husband died of a stroke, you know, years back, but she kept the house. I used to visit her regular. Now they did have a son. Name wasn't David though. George, that was it, just like his father, rest his soul. A big strapping boy he was, basketball star it seems to me. But he'd be older now, wouldn't he, so he's not the one. Wouldn't be anyway, name's not right, is it?"

"No, ma'am. So, no one named Greer ever lived there?"

"Well, I wouldn't say never. But not since Mr.

Wheatly and I came here, and that was just after we were married, fifty-three years ago."

"Well, thank you . . . Mrs. Wheatly. I must have the wrong address or something. Sorry to have bothered you."

"Oh, no bother, young man. Just sorry I couldn't help. We've some smart geneologists down at the museum, though. You might try them."

"Thank you. Yes, I might."

He walked down the path and out the swinging gate. No. No point in trying geneologists for someone who'd clearly been making up his own past. Standing alone on the sidewalk, Dan felt shaken. He hadn't expected this. He thought there might be some old dirt to dig up about the family, but not that there'd be nothing to dig up at all.

The first splattering of rain brought him around. There was a rumbling in the distance that was not traffic. Pulling up his collar, he hurried down the street to where he'd seen a gas station. He'd call a cab there.

Rain fell in a light drizzle, steaming back up from the pavement with a warm wet smell. The kids with their Big Wheels had been called in.

The storm didn't fully break until he was in the cab. He leaned back against the seat. The springs were out, and it smelled of old cigarettes, his wet clothes and years of sweaty passengers. Glumly he looked through the sheets of rain as they bounced and splashed their way to the bus station.

He wished he hadn't started this, hadn't picked up that blasted calculator. The more he learned, or didn't learn, the worse it looked. Watson and Holmes didn't have this problem. Their mysteries were tidy, never touching their own lives. He felt something awful could be building up, something that could break like this storm. But what, he wondered, could he do about it?

Chapter 4

A cheering sign-waving crowd greeted them at the airport. Ben Stratton, followed by his wife and son, stepped from the plane and waved. At the foot of the ramp, the candidate gave a brief speech while salty breezes whipped at his hopelessly tangled hair.

The three Strattons stepped into a gleaming black limousine and were wisked away from the San Francisco airport. Motorcycles screamed ahead of them as they and a fleet of press cars sped into the city.

Sirens still wailing, they finally pulled in front of the St. Francis Hotel, the Stratton Convention headquarters. Another crowd of supporters waved and cheered. Surprised passers-by craned to see which of the candidates this was. Some joined in the cheering. After all, Stratton had won California's primary, not with a majority but with more votes than the other four candidates.

The Strattons stepped from the limousine. Cameras clicked, and people cheered harder. Dan felt both thrilled and ridiculous. But he'd really liked the motorcycles. Inside the lobby, the stately elegance of dark wood, gleaming brass and wine-red carpet were almost obscured by the mob of press and excited supporters bubbling at the chance to see their candidate in person.

On a portable platform bristling with microphones, Senator Stratton gave a brief speech, a variant of the one Dan had heard countless times before. The difference now was the ring of burly secret service men scanning the crowd, their eyes shifting back and forth like mechanical owls.

When at last the family made it to their rooms upstairs, Dan looked hurriedly through the impressive suite. His and his parents' rooms and their own private living room were connected to an even larger suite serving as the Stratton Convention Headquarters. He'd explore later, but now he didn't even take time to unpack.

"Mom," he said heading for the door, "I know there's some function later, but I've still got at least two hours. I'm going to see something of San Francisco while I've got a chance."

"Don't you think one of the secret service men should go with you?"

"No! Hey look, if Dad actually gets elected

President, I won't even be able to go to Baskin and Robbins without one of them. Give me a break."

"All right. Don't get lost, and be back by two— no later."

He fled out the door and down the elevator. In the lobby, no one recognized him without his father. Just another eager kid wearing a Stratton button.

Outside, he chose a direction at random and after a few blocks impulsively jumped a passing cablecar. The thing was jammed with convention delegates playing tourist. A lady with a Kulani button allowed him to crowd in and pay his toll. After a few blocks he hopped off at what appeared to be Chinatown, judging by the upturned eaves and bilingual street signs.

For an hour he explored the streets that ran steeply up and down from Grant Avenue. He poked into shops smelling of incense, whose goods ranged from expensive treasures to cheap tourist junk. His only purchase was a handful of postcards to send to Carla, Dick Lenox and some of his friends in Bloomington. He usually brought back such things unwritten, but he resolved to do better this time. Historic occasion and all.

Hungry now, he tentatively stepped into a grocery store that exuded odd smells and hung even odder things in the windows. He wasn't *that* hungry, he decided, and retreated down the street to a Chinese fast foodery where he bought several large intriguing-smelling pastries.

Taking them to a little park he'd discovered, he sat on a bench under a large statue of Buddha. Across from him, an elderly Chinese gentleman scattered crumbs to greedy, strutting pigeons.

Mechanically Dan chewed and thought. Here it was, almost the climax of the campaign, and he still didn't know what to do with his suspicions. It was dangerous, he knew, to rock the boat now, everything was so delicately balanced. But suppose Greer himself was targeting this time for whatever his scheme was? Or suppose some unfriendlies discovered and used his secret? On the other hand, if he told and Greer withdrew, the whole campaign could collapse. Greer and his computer were important to so much of it.

He knew he was stalling. Acting like Hamlet, indecisive when he should be stabbing somebody. But who, how and when? He needed more pieces to the puzzle. Suddenly, another idea fell into place.

Crumpling up the greasy papers, he tossed them into a trash can. The pigeon feeder had already left, and a few of his flock descended on the can. Dan got up and headed back to Grant Avenue. He had to stop three people before he found a local who could give directions back to the St. Francis.

That afternoon, the family attended a reception for California bigwigs. Amid drinks and lavish hors d'oeuvres, they watched the Convention's keynote address on a big screen.

Afterwards, exhaustion hit Dan like a hammer. The long flight and tense, busy day suddenly caught up with him. Stumbling down the hotel corridor, he accidentally bumped into David Greer. He turned to the little man, gray hair impossibly neat, eyes enigmatic behind wraparound glasses. The frustrations of months suddenly boiled over. Impulsively he said, "Oh, David, I was in Indianapolis the other day. I met Mrs. Wheatly. She sends her regards."

"Mrs. Wheatly?"

"Your old neighbor."

"Um . . . yes. How is she?"

"Fine, but her memory's pretty poor."

Greer stared at him, his face tightening into a mask. Without comment, he turned away.

Dan watched his hurried retreat. You idiot! he thought to himself. What did you do that for? Now he knows you're on to him. He'll probably murder you in your sleep. No, he wouldn't risk that, but he'll be on his guard. And you'd better be too. What an arrogant jerk you are, Dan Stratton!

He slipped by the others at the headquarters suite and went directly to his own room, hardly noticing its poshness. He wasn't at all pleased with himself. Even Dr. Watson wouldn't blunder like that.

Next morning, Mrs. Stratton and Dan, stiff in suit and tie, had to go to the Women's Alliance for something-or-other. Then there was a luncheon for some business organization. The Convention session was to start at 2:00 p.m. so highlights could make prime time TV on the East Coast. Dan decided he'd go. He'd seen conventions on TV since before he could walk. It would be fun to actually be there.

It was only a few blocks to the convention hall, a huge concrete bunker sunk partway underground. Out front of the hall, against the brilliant blue sky, a row of huge flags snapped in the breeze. Demonstrators for and against various causes mingled with button and souvenir salesmen. Stopped at a police barricade, Dan fumbled around in his jacket for his credentials.

"Better wear it around your neck, son," the policeman said letting him by.

Reluctantly he hung the cord about his neck. The big paper tag dangling in front made him feel like a piece of furniture at a clearance sale.

Once inside, he was herded through a metal detector, down escalators and through another credentials check and another. The last guard gave him a look as though someone his age couldn't possibly have a VIP guest pass. Two more checks, and he was on the convention floor. This certainly wasn't a place to slip in for a lark.

The session had already begun, and speeches were wafting forth largely unheard. People were still pouring in, and it seemed that for every delegate, there were at least two press people pursuing news, rumors, celebrities or photos. For once he was glad to be completely undistinguished looking.

He wandered through the noisy, jostling crowd until he found the Indiana delegation. A few familiar people greeted him warmly and immediately began jabbering at him. Only half listening, he sat back and tried to absorb the whole scene.

It struck him immediately what it looked like. The great arched ceiling was crisscrossed with girders and hundreds of blazing high-powered spotlights. It was the set of a science fiction movie. The huge outer-space drydock for repairing the *Enterprise*. This one sight was worth the trip to San Francisco, though he didn't know how it would do as a setting for his father, given the space issue.

Speeches were now being made about the platform planks, statements of party policy on various issues. The podium rose from the sea of delegates like a Biblestory picture of the Tower of Babel (an appropriate analogy, Dan thought). Across it paraded the party's major figures, and applause rolled in waves over the floor as one side or another scored oratorical points.

Dan got up and made his way to the back of the hall, searching for the Stratton communications center. Eventually he found it, a partitioned off area around an oversized trailer. Young volunteers hurried importantly about with buckets of buttons, stapled signs, or strained to hear walkie-talkie messages from floor workers.

Dan made himself useful sorting pages of policy statements, all the while keeping an eye on Greer.

Though he didn't know what he expected—to have the little man suddenly whip out a machine gun and mow everyone down?

Greer's metalic lenses reflected the chaotic scene around him as he calmly alternated between talking on a phone and working with his calculator. Dan wondered which screen he was using and why. He really wished he hadn't mentioned Mrs. Wheatly. It was probably just the glasses, but the guy looked like he could be ruthless.

Out on the convention floor, votes were being taken on the platform planks. The staff examined each result like ancient soothsayers examining entrails, and predicted what it meant for each candidate's chances. Things, Dan gathered, weren't decisive for them, but at least they weren't depressing.

Again Dan wandered out over the floor, watching the hoopla and wolfing down a taco for dinner. Political bigwigs he'd seen in plenty, but he was thrilled to actually rub shoulders with some of the network celebrities as, with detached expressions they plowed their way through the crowds. Dan stayed until the last gavel clanked down, then poured out with the other weary delegates and attached himself to some Stratton staffers trudging back to the St. Francis.

For a while afterwards, he lounged around the Stratton inner sanctum munching doughnuts and sleepily listening as McKenzie discussed the "secret mission" he'd made to the LaSalle camp last night.

Halfway through, the phone rang. Lederman answered and after a moment handed it to Senator Stratton mouthing, "This is it."

His dad said a few yesses and noes into the phone, then gave those in the room a big grin and thumbs up sign. "Great, Phil," he said into the receiver. "Good to have you aboard. Now we'll see if we can make this thing float." He was silent again, then replied, "Yes, I understand. To carry the analogy further, if the damned thing runs aground, it's every man for himself. Agreed." Silence. "Good. Then we'll get things rolling on this end. Thanks, Phil. Good night."

He hung up, and the room exploded in cheering. "We've got a fighting chance now!" Lederman exclaimed over the din. "Adding those LaSalle votes to ours brings us mighty close. Particularly after those economy and space plank votes tonight. We've got floating support out there somewhere."

The room settled down as the campaign manager continued. "David's been calculating where those weak points are, and that's where we start our rumor mongering. Start spreading the word—unofficially mind you—that LaSalle's agreed to be Ben's Vice-President and is throwing his votes to us. David, your turn."

Dan got up and slipped out to his bedroom. He didn't want to hear Greer's briefing. And he had no intention of spending his morning spreading calculated rumors. He was planning a secret mission of his own.

The following morning, he caught his mother as she was rushing out and told her he was going across the Bay to Berkeley to see a really important exhibit on the prehistory of California.

She kissed his cheek absently and said, "Have a good time, dear." He suspected he could have said he was going to Honolulu for a belly dancers' conference and she would have said the same. But he had what he needed.

The Bay Area Rapid Transit, BART, station was near the hotel. Once there, he found the system reassuringly like the Washington Metro, but it still took a while studying maps to work up the courage to stick his money in a slot. Ticket in hand, he stood on the underground platform waiting for what he hoped was the right train, until the sleek monster roared out of the earth and carried him deep under the rock and waters of the bay.

San Francisco had been shrouded in morning fog; but when he emerged from the station at Berkeley, the sky was clear and sunny. Asking the way to the University campus, he headed off. He had called Professor Erhardt day before yesterday, after returning from Chinatown, and made an appointment. Now as he entered the campus he rehearsed his story and looked about.

Morning sun slanted through a grove of towering eucalyptus, their blue-gray trunks looking like pillars of some ancient temple. He wished trees like this grew in Indiana. The campus buildings varied in style, but all were designed to impress with the majesty of learning. They were, he thought, fairly successful.

Professor Erhardt proved to be a big man with an even bigger beard. He looked like a sooty Santa Claus, except that his eyes definitely did not twinkle. Dan imagined his classes in astrophysics would be no treat.

"Professor Erhardt," he began nervously, once he was seated, "thank you for seeing me on such short notice. As I said, I've been helping put together a paper for my father's campaign on the sorts of academic research that would *not* be hurt by cutbacks in the space program. There's thinking around that my father's opposed to all research—and he's not. He just opposes using our limited resources on space gadgetry when there is so much human need on Earth." That was lifted right out of a speech, and Dan feared it sounded ludicrously stilted coming from him.

"Yes, I understand your concern . . . Mr. Stratton." Dan hated the faintly patronizing smirk, but pretended not to notice. "And you want me to give you a rundown on projects on this campus that would be unaffected?"

"That's right, sir. Your name was suggested to me by a member of our staff, David Greer. No doubt you remember him, he took several graduate seminars from you about ten years ago. He recommends you highly."

"Greer? David Greer, you say? I don't recall the name."

Dan tensed as if to pounce on his prey. "Let me describe him, he's very distinctive-looking. Rather short and thin. His hair's gray, though maybe it wasn't then. And he hurt his eyes in the army before coming to Berkeley and wears dark glasses all the time."

"No, I don't recall him, I'm afraid, and I usually do remember my graduate students. But never mind, I appreciate his remembering me. Now as to those projects, yes, I can give you an overview."

The professor launched into a long detailed discussion, and Dan dutifully took notes. Long notes. He wished he'd thought this through a little better. Now he was stuck scribbling for an hour and a half, when he already had the information he needed. Oh well, he'd made the whole thing up, but maybe someone could actually write a paper on it.

When he finally excused himself from the professor, his brain was swimming with statistics. But in the center lay one cold hard fact. David Greer's official past was a tissue of lies. And he alone knew it.

He'd planned to find the student bookstore and buy something on California archaeology to skim as a cover for this trip. But he imagined he could make up any trash and his parents would accept it just now.

He was getting depressingly good at concocting lies these days.

Fighting lies with lies; the nature of politics, he thought bitterly. But this thing was really too big for what his dad called easy cynicism. He knew that with certainty now. But another uncertainty tormented him. He still didn't know what to do about it.

Chapter 5

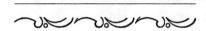

Dan got off at the BART station nearest the convention hall and walked there directly. This was nomination night, and if anything, the noise and chaos inside was worse than before. After helping pass out armloads of "Stratton for President" signs, he drifted off, trying to lose his tension in the excitement of the crowd.

A barrel-shaped senator recognized him and slammed him on the shoulder, bellowing above the clamor, "Well, how does it feel to have your dad this close to being President?"

"Just great, sir." He smiled weakly while people around them swiveled to see this apparent celebrity. As he slipped away, he heard a voice answer another behind him, "Well, I'd look worried too if my father were going through this. Poor kid."

Poor kid, indeed, he thought as he finally sank into an empty aisle seat in the Alabama delegation. He did want his dad to win. Desperately. Mainly because he knew how much his dad wanted it—not because being President was a barrel of laughs, but because Ben Stratton deeply believed in what he said. Maybe, Dan thought, it was a good thing he had this other worry, or he'd be so concerned now over the nomination he'd have chewed his fingers to the bone.

He looked around him and saw he had sunk into a forest of hand-made "Stratton-LaSalle" signs. Besides him, a big woman was wearing a straw wastepaper basket on her head. It was festooned with buttons and little flags. The ample front of her dress glittered with more decorations than a four-star general. Most of the buttons were for LaSalle.

A young man leaned across him to talk to the woman. "Mary Lou, you got the word about our boy and Stratton?"

"Yes, sugar, many times." She patted the young man's arm with a beringed hand. "And I'm a team player, if it's a winning team."

Dan slipped away from the lady with the hat. She'd decorated herself to attract network cameras, and he felt too transparent and brittle to be on TV just now.

Wandering toward the back of the hall and the

official souvenir stands, he considered buying some mementoes. But he didn't see anything he thought Carla might like, and besides, he thought, she was lucky he'd remembered to send the postcard.

He was moving on when a news commentator and camera crew shoved through the crowded aisle to where the view opened onto the convention floor, colorful with flags and bobbing signs. He tried to get away, but was crushed between a delegate's ample beer belly and a camera backpack. The lights blazed on, and the cool blonde lady, looking slightly insectoid with a single antenna sticking up from her earphones, smiled and came alive, as if suddenly switched on.

"Yes, this is the Convention's day of decision. Across the floor rumors are flying, bargains are being made or broken, and arms are being twisted. In a few hours . . ."

Wriggling free, Dan ducked under a rope and hurried away. This was his day of decision, too; and he had just made it. He'd tell them what he knew. Not his father, he had enough worries now, but McKenzie.

First though, he'd need some solid physical evidence, not just verbal holes in Greer's past. The best thing would be Greer's calculator, but he didn't see how he'd get hold of that, short of tackling the nasty little guy. But he thought he knew where else to try.

Purposeful now, he headed to the Stratton trailer. Greer was there talking to a man with a big LaSalle button. He looked up, but Dan lowered his gaze and slipped away.

He hurried two steps at a time up the slowly rising escalator and rushed out of the hall. Taxis clustered about, but on these crowded streets he figured it would be quicker to walk. Slowing down only as he entered the hotel lobby, he headed decisively to the front desk, allowing himself no time for second thoughts.

The young man behind the desk finished dealing with an elderly couple and turned to him. Dan smiled broadly.

"Hello, I'm Dan Stratton. I'm supposed to share a room tonight with David Greer, but he forgot to give me a key."

The man looked at him a moment then consulted some files. "I have you down as sharing the suite with your parents."

"Right, but my dad's sister came into town today, and they offered her my room. David said I could use the extra bed in his but forgot to give me the keys. I'll never find him on the convention floor, it's so crowded. And my mom said to go move my stuff out of Aunt Laura's way."

He ended with what he hoped was a pathetic smile. The man studied him another moment. "All right, Mr. Stratton. I see your problem." He dropped the keys into his hand.

Dan thanked him and hurried to the elevator, emotions bouncing between self-loathing and self-congratulations. Well, he said to himself finally, you work with what you've got.

Upstairs, he walked swiftly to Greer's room. He knew it'd been a safe bet that the disagreeable man had no roommates. The key fitted smoothly. He opened the door and closed it firmly behind him.

Switching on the light, he took a deep breath and surveyed the room. There must be something incriminating here. He wished he knew how the FBI did this sort of thing.

A half-empty suitcase lay open on a luggage rack. The obvious place to start. He checked carefully through the things inside, trying to get nothing out of order. It was all very ordinary. Clothing. Nothing with labels saying "Made in Moscow." Idiot, he thought to himself, what do you expect? Nothing in the pockets, and he couldn't find any secret compartments.

Next he checked through the clothes hanging in the closet, then went through the drawers. Pajamas, underwear, and nothing else besides the hotel-issued Bible, stationery and dining guides. He thought of looking under the mattress, but decided that Greer wouldn't hide anything there because a maid did the bed every day.

He looked behind curtains and mirrors, under lamps and chairs. Nothing. Then he went into the bathroom. Besides the hotel's towels, glasses and soap, there was a yellow toothbrush, toothpaste and a box of coughdrops. He opened this and smelled. Coughdrops. There were also several labelless jars of cream and what appeared to be a roll of tape. He pulled a little loose, but it was definitely sticky tape and not the recording kind. The jars he opened, and tentatively stuck a finger into the whitish cream inside. It smelled vaguely of pineapple. He rubbed a little on the back of his hand, but that told him nothing. Then he turned the jars over, checking them for false bottoms. Again nothing.

He stood back and looked at the sink again. There really was nothing of interest there. An ordinary man's bathroom. Yet something seemed missing. What? He tried to picture his dad's sink. Of course. There was no shaving equipment! His flush of discovery immediately faded. So the guy probably used an electric razor and had it with him now to fight off five o'clock shadow.

Discouraged, Dan returned to the bedroom and leafed through a stack of papers on the bureau. There was a list of which hotels delegations were housed in, and an invitation to a reception the mayor of San Francisco had held last Saturday. Nothing not in English, no list of "contacts," not even a scrap of paper with a mysterious address. And no weird symbols. One file marked "Confidential, take to Convention Floor" excited him at first, but proved to be nothing but signed vote pledges from non-Stratton delegates. Important, but not to him.

Dan sighed and decided to take one last look through the suitcase. He was lifting out a stack of shirts, when suddenly the door opened. David Greer stood there staring at him. Dropping the shirts, Dan dashed for the door. Greer slammed it closed and gripped the boy's shoulders. Panicking, Dan reached up, grabbing his arms and pushed Greer aside.

To his horror, this small exertion flung the man clear across the room. He slammed against the wall, knocking of his glasses, then slumped groggily to the floor.

Talk about your ninety-eight pound weakling, Dan thought, this guy's more like twenty-eight pounds!

Holding a hand over his eyes, Greer scrabbled over the floor feeling for his glasses. A large grayish bruise was already appearing on his cheek where he'd hit the wall.

Dan felt like a triple heel. Throw a near-blind runt against the wall, beat him up and knock off his glasses! Might as well stomp on them while you're at it. You're a real jerk, Dan Stratton.

He stepped over and kicked the glasses toward the other's groping hand. "Here."

Grabbing them, Greer slipped them on and looked up. His cheek was looking considerably worse.

"Sorry," Dan blurted out. "I was just looking for something. I'll go now." He moved to the door.

"No, don't go!" Greer said standing up shakily. "Obviously we've got to talk."

"I'll talk, but not to you."

"No. No, you must. Please don't go yet. It could ruin everything!" His voice was high and desperate, the accent stronger.

Dan hesitated. "What do you have to say?" he asked at last.

Sitting wearily on the bed, Greer motioned Dan to a chair. He looked at the boy a moment. "You have some reason to suspect me. What was it? The calculator?"

"That and the fact that the army has no record of your medical treatments, and that you never lived at that address in Indianapolis or took the courses on your college transcripts."

Greer groaned. "The army records were a slip-up on my part, all right. But one can't alter people's memories. You've been very thorough, Danny. I underestimated you. Have you told anyone else about this?"

"Why? So you can decide if it's safe to rub me out?"

"No. I've done a lot of strange things, but I draw the line at murder. Now that you've learned this much, I'm clearly going to have to tell you the whole story. But the fewer people who know, the better. That includes McKenzie and your father. Particularly your father."

"If you think I'm going to let you—"

"Danny, believe me, I would do nothing to harm your father or his chances for the Presidency. That's the goal I've worked for all these years."

"Sure you've worked for him. But you've never shown you liked him—or any of us."

Standing up, Greer paced over to the window,

then looked back. "I know. That was part of the plan. Try to keep people from getting close enough to see the holes in my identity. Obviously, it backfired. But believe me, Danny, there's nothing evil in what I'm doing.

"So, start telling me about it."

The other gestured helplessly in the air. "I can't. Not now. It's a long, complex story, and there's no time. I have work to do right now. Besides, there're things I have in Washington that you'll need to understand it."

"If you think I'm taking you on faith, forget it!" Dan stood up angrily. "There's work I have to do now, too."

"Danny, stop playing the hero! This is the real world. Okay, suppose you go right in and tell your father one of his chief aide's a phony. What happens?"

"If he believes me, he fires you."

"Exactly. And what does that do to his campaign?"

Dan was silent.

"He needs me. If I go, it could sabotage his whole campaign."

"You'd wipe the computer!"

"I could, but I wouldn't. I want him to win. But if he finds out about me, I'd have to leave. And besides, rumor would get out; there'd be scandal. One way or another, your father would lose."

"You're blackmailing me!"

"I am not! I'm telling you the truth. Keep silent

a few days, and I promise you two things. First, nothing I am doing will harm your father, his chances at the Presidency, or this country. And second, if you come to my Washington apartment as soon as we're all back there, I'll tell you and show you everything."

Dan scowled. "I haven't much choice, have I?"

"I hope not. This is too important."

"All right, but if you do anything to . . ."

"Danny, if anything goes wrong, if we lose, tell the world about me if you want. It won't matter then."

Greer stood up, wincing as he touched a finger to his bruised face. "This probably looks as bad as it feels." Walking into the bathroom he stared into the mirror, then opening a jar he daubed cream on his face. When he came out, the gray blotch was hidden.

Greer straightened his tie and took the "confidential" file off the bureau. "If I'd trusted someone else to come back for this—"

"I'd have told what I knew anyway."

Nodding, Greer walked to the door, then turned back. "I'll keep my word, Danny. For your father's sake, for all our sakes, keep yours."

Seething and confused, Dan watched the little man hurry down the hall. Whatever Greer's game was, this certainly wasn't the sort of scene he might have expected. Frowning, he stepped out of the room, locking the door behind him.

He was angry, angry at Greer and angry at himself. But there was a touch of relief, too. He'd accepted a bargain—or submitted to blackmail. But either way, action had been taken, a decision made. And for a few days, the ball was in another court.

He headed down the hall. Maybe he'd watch the rest of the session on TV with his parents. Then he slowed. He really couldn't face his dad just now. He had just done something major to his campaign. But whether it was a boost or a death blow, he didn't know.

Dejected, he headed instead down the elevator and back to the convention hall. If one wanted a crowd to lose oneself in, that was certainly provided.

As he dropped into an empty seat in the Indiana delegation, Dan realized they'd already started Stratton nominating speeches. He forced himself to listen. The fiery rhetoric and electric excitement around him slowly burned away his gloom. Soon he was applauding enthusiastically at all the right points. When the last speech ended, he leaped up with the rest, screaming and cheering, waving a sign and marching around the floor. Everywhere, he saw grown men and women making no less fools of themselves. But politics, he knew, was a large part acting, and those around him were political artists.

Afterwards he felt better than he had in days.

Finally, after the same routine was gone through for Vonderman, the voting began. As Alabama's name was called, a realization hit Dan like a physical blow. This was it. The climax of everything. All those speeches, all those handshakes, all those long, weary hours of planning and traveling. All those people around the country who had worked so hard for a man most had never even met. And maybe whatever Greer was up to, too. All had been building toward this.

And for the first time in months, Dan knew just how much he wanted his father to win. He felt sick and didn't want to be on public view. Practically running to the trailer compound, he made himself small in a corner and watched the big board where young helpers with earphones were marking up the states' votes as fast as they were given.

Faces around him were stony at first, but slowly began warming with a flush of hope. They picked up a few votes here or there that they hadn't expected. In Colorado, Vonderman was down four votes from his projection. Kulani's vote didn't hold in Massachusetts. Most of Michigan's Babcock delegates swung to Stratton.

The numbers mounted closer and closer to the total needed. The air around them tingled. Vonderman carried the Washington delegation, but West Virginia added twenty-eight of its forty-five votes to the Stratton column. Wisconsin. This could be it!

"Madam Chairman," the voice entoned over the booming microphone, "the great state of Wisconsin proudly casts five votes for our good neighbor from Michigan, George Babcock, eight votes for Congress-

woman Kulani, thirty-six votes for Senator Vonderman, and its remaining forty-one votes for the next
President of the United States, Benjamin K. Stratton!"

The hall exploded in sound. They were two votes
over the top. His dad had won! Everywhere around
him people were leaping and hugging and crying and
laughing. He hugged people he didn't know. A thin
hand grabbed his and shook it. He looked into the
man's smiling face and realized that, for the moment,
he even liked David Greer.

Hours later, after much noise, happiness and cele-
bration, Dan crawled between the clean, cool sheets
of his bed. The reality of it all was slowly sinking in.
His dad was really the nominee! He just might beat
Fred Hambly in November. Next year he could be
President of the United States. It was ridiculous and
frightening, but it was deliriously exciting too, and
that was enough for the present. Tired and very
happy, he fell asleep.

Chapter 6

Washington, DC, being used to monumental events, was not vibrating with excitement as much as Dan thought it should. But the Stratton home certainly was. The phone rang constantly; people came and went at all hours; and his dad seldom got to sit down for more than a minute. The three Strattons were intensely glad that Senator Karstell had invited them for a week of rest and recuperation on his Idaho ranch. They would leave in a few days, as soon as expanded staff appointments were made.

Dan had not forgotten his own appointment. Nervously, he hung around the fringes of a staff meeting at his house, pretending to be absorbed in a book about Roman Britain.

Finally the book did get interesting, and he jumped like a cricket when Greer stepped quietly behind his chair and dropped a piece of paper into his book.

Feeling as though fifty concealed cameras were trained on him, he read the message. "10:00 a.m. tomorrow," it said simply and gave Greer's address.

After a minute, Dan closed his book and walked quietly up to his room. For a long while he sat at his desk thinking, then deliberately he got out a notebook and began writing. As accurately as he could, he wrote down everything he had discovered about Greer —the weird calculator and all the holes in his past.

Leaning back, he looked the paper over. This was a pretty flimsy indictment, he realized. Given that adults seldom credit a kid with important discoveries, most of this could probably be explained away. But there was Greer's confession at the hotel. That clinched things. As an addition, he wrote down every word of that he could remember, including the invitation to go to Greer's apartment for the rest of the story. Then he slipped the sheets into an envelope, sealed it and wrote "to be opened if I'm not home in two days." Dating it, he signed his full name, Daniel Christopher Stratton.

He looked around the room for someplace to put it, someplace his mother wouldn't find it casually if she thought to tidy his room. But what do mothers do when they learn that their son has been murdered? Look at his old toys? Go cry on his pillow?

Now he was getting morbid—and ridiculous, too. Greer wouldn't kill him, not if he wanted continued secrecy. Murder of a presidential candidate's son would be well investigated. He smiled wryly. There were compensations.

Finally he tucked the envelope under his old teddy bear on the windowsill and resolved not to be melodramatic for the rest of the day. He'd go out to the driveway and shoot a few baskets. Or maybe Chuck down the street wanted to go bicycling to one of the parks.

At four minutes to ten the next morning, Dan stood outside a tall, modern apartment building. Every step he'd taken there had weighed him more heavily with dread. Almost certainly he was walking into a trap. Dumb heroes in movies did that all the time, but they also had the powers and special effects to get themselves out again.

He looked at the elegantly uniformed doorman. This place was posh. Maybe Greer got Mafia money. The accent might be Italian.

The doorman was elderly but strikingly tall, obviously intended to intimidate rather than guard. Dan felt plenty intimidated. He gave the man his name and the number of the apartment he wished to visit. The other pressed a button, and in a moment a tinny voice from a grill said he was expected. With a nod, the man opened the door.

Well, Dan thought glumly, at least someone had

seen him enter. If he never came out, this old guy might remember, when the police questioned him.

He went to the elevator and, once inside, pressed the number for the top floor. Posher and posher. The hall was thickly carpeted. He padded quietly over it looking for the right number. Finding it, he stopped and stared at the door, wondering what was on the other side. Thirty thugs with machine guns? A vat of black widow spiders? Shakily he tapped the buzzer.

The door opened. David Greer stood there looking perfectly ordinary with an ordinary apartment around him. As he stepped in, Dan noted that the one extraordinary feature was the incredible view. One wall of the front room was a floor to ceiling window looking out over the whole majestic expanse of central Washington. The glass was so clean, it seemed there was no barrier at all. An uneasiness with heights kept Dan on the far side of the room.

"Have a seat, Danny," Greer said. "But you prefer 'Dan' don't you?"

Dan nodded, selecting a vibrant blue jell-chair. He liked this modern form-fitting furniture, but his mother resolutely stuck with Early American. A tray of orange juice rested on the coffee table. Dan looked at it doubtfully.

Greer smiled. "No, it's not drugged. Just an attempt at hospitality. I'm not used to this."

Dan picked one glass, and taking the other, Greer sat opposite him on an orange plastic couch.

"Well, Dan," he said leaning back, "you've obviously found your vocation, private investigator. Or maybe I just didn't cover my tracks too well. Filling computers with false information was easy, except for the medical slip-up. But real people can't be made to remember things as easily as machines.

"Was it all fake then?"

"Everything. Growing up in Indianapolis, the army, all those good grades at Berkeley, even the eye injury." He raised a hand to his dark glasses. "The light does bother me, but I wear these mainly for disguise."

Slowly he took off the glasses. Had Dan's chair been less encompassing, he would have fallen off of it. Greer's eyes were totally inhuman. Round like an owl's, they had no pupils. Tiny flecks of gold floated in deep silver pools.

Greer spoke calmly. "You see, I only came to this planet, the surface that is, nine years ago. Actually I arrived at the orbiting research station some six years earlier. Just a naïve grad student of his first field project. In anthropology, you'd say. The Council's had a station here since the nineteen thirties studying the culture through broadcasts and detailed photography."

Dan realized he was staring with his mouth hanging open like a fish. He shut it.

Greer continued, looking out the window, the light glancing off the specks in his eyes. "It was supposed to be just a short research stint. Ha! The problem was that the Council had been studying our data and concluded that your culture was a class forty-three, critically imbalanced type. Shortly before I was to leave, word came through that they'd decided on intervention."

"What d'ya mean?" Dan croaked out, proud he could say anything.

"Well, most cultures in the galaxy develop in an integrated way. Technological advances more or less go along with ethical and cultural ones. But in some species one side outstrips the other. They might be very intelligent with a highly developed moral sense, but in terms of technology be on the level of ox carts and flint knives. Or it could be the other way, a very advanced technology with little moral judgment to control it."

"And we're like that?"

"Definitely. Your inability to rationally use nuclear power is only the most obvious example."

"But what's this about intervention? If we want to blow ourselves up, that's our problem, isn't it?"

"Certainly. And many cultures have done it. It would be a shame, but as you say, it's your problem. It becomes our problem, however, when an unbalanced culture like yours is also on the verge of getting into space with the rest of us. Not that your weapons are any threat, but the whole erratic nature of your culture is. History shows that when a species like yours joins the interstellar community, it causes waves of disruption that eventually must be dealt with—usually unpleasantly."

"So, what are you going to do? Come in and wipe us out?"

"Not necessary. The usual policy is to intervene before that stage is reached and set up a protectorate, sort of an interstellar ward."

"And that's what you're doing here?"

"No! That's what I'm trying to prevent! We anthropologists don't like intervention. Once a primitive culture like yours becomes a galactic protectorate, it almost always loses its identity. Young cultures are so impressionable and eager to adopt the new ways that they abandon their old ways—whatever it was that made them special. We felt that if you could be left to ripen on your own, you'd have a lot to contribute to galactic culture itself."

He paused a moment. "Does this make any sense to you?"

Dan frowned. "What you're worried about is what happened to primitive people here when Europeans came—sort of getting absorbed and forgotten?"

"Exactly. You'll make an anthropologist yet."

"But I still don't understand . . ."

"What I'm doing here? Well, we got permission to try some selective intervention. Your actual development of interstellar travel was some years off. So it was hoped that if we could step in and influence events away from that development, it would give you time to get your cultural act together, so to speak.

"I was chosen because I'd studied the culture and languages longer than anyone else and because my species is basically bipedal— easier to pass off as human.

"The critical research was more advanced in this country, and analysis showed that events here could be most profoundly influenced through the political process, so we—"

"Wait a minute!" Dan spat out. "Are you saying that my dad is just a tool for a bunch of funny-eyed space students?"

"Hey, no. Don't get worked up! Your dad was chosen because he was already speaking out on the space issue and because he had the best prospects of advancing to the Presidency. I just did what I could to strengthen his commitment and improve his chances."

"Your computer work . . . ?"

"Right, that's one tactic. The information in that campaign computer is so thorough because a lot comes from our sources. My calculator is the tie-in. But that's enough talking. I've got something to show you."

Greer got up and walked over to an interior wall. Hestitantly Dan followed. Splayed across the wall's edge was a modern sculpture of tangled bronze leaves. Greer pressed one leaf and a small dark patch appeared in the wall, expanding rapidly, like rippling water, into a large oval opening.

As Greer stepped through, light came on in the room beyond, a hazy green light like that in an aquarium. Dan followed him in growing bewilderment.

The center of the inner room was dominated by a large translucent cylinder rising from floor to ceiling. A silver ring a foot high encircled its base, small knobs studding the surface at irregular intervals.

Some sort of console ran the length of one wall, humming with a deep almost inaudible purr. Between clusters of knobs, oddly tinted light played over the surface like heat lightning. One end of the console wrapped around a large clear bubble filled with violet light. Inside lay an ordinary book, its pages turning rapidly.

Dan stared at it. "What's that?"

"A copier. Working on a book of Central Asia folklore, I believe. One advantage of having an agent on the planet's surface is that we're no longer limited to remote research. We're trying to preserve what we can, hedging our bets in case this does become a dead culture."

Greer stepped to the central cylinder and seated himself amid a mass of reddish filaments that circled it on the floor. "Have a seat. I'll contact the station."

Cautiously Dan poked a toe at the nestlike stuff, as if testing ice water. Then slowly he sat down among its strands. Gently they engulfed the lower half of his body, giving, yet supporting him in every move he made. It was comfortable, but he was still too confused to really enjoy it.

Greer ran his hands over the knobs along the base, and a pinkish glow spread up the cylinder, dissolving into a three-dimensional scene.

They appeared to be looking into a tall, narrow room with rounded corners. One wall was lined from floor to ceiling with unfamiliar instruments, and halfway up a creature was clinging. Covered in what seemed to be gray fur, it hung effortlessly by one arm, and stretched out another to adjust a knob. As it reached, Dan saw leathery wings hanging loosely from the arms. The creature deftly moved its long prehensile tail toward another control, twisting it with the lozenge-shaped pad on the tail tip.

Greer pressed a knob in front of him, and a faint chime sounded in the room into which they looked. The creature on the wall looked around with a small trilling exclamation and let go. Wings outstretched, it glided down to the floor near the viewers.

"That's my sister," Greer said, a tinge of unmistakable pride in his voice. "My twin actually."

Startled, Dan looked at his companion. His hair, that they'd always thought prematurely gray, *was* the same steely shade as that creature's fur. Had he actually been born, or hatched, or whatever, with hair like that all over?

Dan was just absorbing this when Greer uttered a series of rapid screeching chirps mixed with glutteral growls. The sounds, so profoundly inhuman, killed Dan's last doubts. This was no elaborate special-effects hoax. It was all too real.

Turning to Dan again, Greer switched abruptly to English, the faint accent now very understandable. "My sister gives you her greetings, but I'm the only linguist in the family, I'm afraid. Actually, I think she just uses that as an excuse so she won't have to take off her hair and come down here."

He turned back to the cylinder. "Ah, here comes Klragul." The word was pronounced with a strange gargle, strange but no more so than the creature that apparently went with it. Entering through a newly appeared doorway was a rust-colored tubular creature. It moved by alternately extending and retracting the fleshy filaments that covered its body. It progressed with apparent indifference to up and down, finally bringing itself erect by greatly extending the filaments at one end of the body. At the upraised end, nestled amid a fringe of bristles, a turquoise membrane pulsed back and forth emiting a deep gargling. Greer responded in a higher-pitched imitation.

After a minute's interchange, Greer returned his attention to Dan. "Actually Klragul is a neighbor of yours—from the Delta Pavonis system. The station's rather understaffed at the moment; the project's uncertainty hasn't encouraged many students. We do have one other now, but they say he's in a rest period —a very profound state with his species. He's a very intelligent, likable fellow. I hope you have a chance to meet him sometime."

Dan wasn't at all sure he shared that hope. It was one thing, seeing creatures like this in comic books, and quite another having them before you and knowing that they were actually circling somewhere over your head.

The bristly creature was speaking again. Greer translated. "He says he is honored to finally meet a member of your species. And he hopes most sincerely that our activities will succeed and your world retain its full independence."

"Oh . . . yes," Dan said, then realized he should make some formal reply. Etiquette books were useless here. "Tell him . . . tell him I am also honored to meet him . . . and, uh . . . I appreciate his concern."

"Spoken like a true politician," Greer said. Dan was too numb to feel the barb.

The winged sister now joined the conversation, ending with a warbling trill that sounded suspiciously like a giggle. Greer snapped something in reply and abruptly ran his hands over the controls, dissolving the picture into fading pink haze.

"What was that last?" Dan inquired.

"Oh, she said they got a big kick out of seeing me on TV at the Convention, trying hard to keep away from the cameramen."

"They watched the Convention?"

"Oh yes, avidly. All Earth transmissions are monitored automatically, but they can watch any they choose."

Dan was staggered. That the American public should watch that circus was bad enough, but to have it followed by a bat-lady, a walking hair curler and a who-knows what asleep in the other room, was almost more than he could bear.

"Let's go back to the other room," Greer said,

standing up from the wiry nest. "You probably don't find this light very comfortable."

Dan hadn't realized how true that was until they stepped through the oval portal into the warm yellow sunlight that flooded through the window, with its familiar earthly scene beyond. Shakily he sank into one of the chairs.

Greer took his dark glasses from the coffee table and replaced them on his face. "The view I've gotten to like, but the light still bothers me." He walked over to the glass wall and looked out.

"You know, Dan," he said after a minute, "if I'd tried, I probably could have made up some cock and bull story about myself that you would have believed. But I decided to tell you the truth—for a reason."

"Oh?" Dan looked steadily at him.

Greer turned back to the view. "I'm going to need your help, Dan."

At this point Dan felt nothing could surprise him. He just waited.

"There have been new developments," Greer continued quietly, "things that have thrown off our careful timetable. If we don't take direct action soon, your dad will lose—we'll all lose."

Dan considered a moment. "I'm willing to help if I can," he said at last. "What do you have in mind?"

"Sabotage."

Chapter 7

"Sabotage? Now wait a minute!" Dan jumped to his feet. "I'm not going to get involved in anything like that!"

Greer sighed, perching himself in a distinctly nonhuman fashion on the back of a chair. "Just let me explain. As I said, the biggest advances in faster than light theory were being made in this country. Mostly they revolved around the work of Dr. Jacob Svengard. He proposed the existence of a type of energy that travels at supra-luminal speeds and that is readily converted into matter. It's rather complex scientifically, and I'm certainly no physicist. Just say that any object converted into this energy automatically travels at faster then light speeds until reconverted into matter at a predetermined point.

"For years the scientific community here rejected Svengard's theories, but he persisted and several years ago received a small research grant. Then last year, President Wainwright's science advisors must suddenly have grasped the significance of this, for they started channeling massive federal funds into the project—secretly, of course, in case the scoffers were right."

"But why was it so important to Wainwright?"

"Because, and I suppose this is a compliment, of all the candidates that could have been put up against Hambly, the one Wainwright most feared was your father. His Earth First message seemed the biggest threat. The polls show voters losing interest in the space program. But, if before the election, Wainwright and his stand-in Hambly could offer the voters the stars—not just orbiting around in tin boxes, but zooming off like Luke Skywalker—then they'd have everyone right back with them."

"And that would mean," Dan said slowly, "my dad would lose, and your people would move right in and turn us into a colony."

"Yes, that is what it would mean. It's just as your dad and Hambly have both been saying, this election does poses a question of destiny."

"But I still don't understand—"

"Dan, because of the federal money, the timetable on the critical test of Svengard's theory has been moved up to a few weeks from now. I don't have time to infiltrate that project. But you happen to know someone who has access to the research facility."

"I do?"

"Your friend Carla Brenner. Her mother is out in Nevada now working on the Svengard Project."

Suddenly Dan felt cold and ill. "Surely you don't expect me to ask Carla to walk in and bomb the place?"

"No. No, what I need is someone to bring back enough information about the physical layout for me to get inside and alter the test mechanism. If it appears that the test failed because of a basic flaw in theory, not only will it become useless to the Hambly campaign, the whole concept will be dismissed for years to come."

Dan got up and paced about the room, well back from the window. "Yes, I can see all that . . . I think. But how am I going to convince Carla? I mean she's a friend! She's not going to be too keen about sabotaging her mother's place of work."

"I don't know how to do it, Dan. You know her. Explain things to her. Bring her here if you want. But you've got to try. As far as I can see, it's our only chance. You dad's only chance."

Fifteen minutes later, Dan was walking along the reassuringly human sidewalks of Washington. But his mind was far from the sights and the bustling crowd. What was he going to do? Call Carla and say a little winged man from outer space wants her to blow up her mother's lab? Lots of luck.

No, he'd have to try explaining in person, someplace where nobody would overhear. He crossed the street to a public phone and pulled from his wallet the wadded-up piece of paper with Carla's number. He wasn't about to make this call at home.

The phone rang twice, and Carla answered; the voices of smaller children screeched in the background. "Hello, Carla, it's Dan."

"Dan! Thanks for the postcard. I bet you had a terrific time. And congratulations by the way. I was rooting for you. Even saw you on TV."

Yeah, he thought, you and who else. He shivered. "Carla, I've got something pretty important to tell you."

"Okay, shoot."

"No, I can't now, not on the phone. It's also sort of secret. Could you, uh . . . meet me someplace tomorrow. Someplace public maybe . . . say the Jefferson Memorial?"

"Wow, cloak and dagger stuff. All right, I'm intrigued. What time?"

"How's ten o'clock?" Cloak and ray gun seemed more appropriate, Dan thought as he hung up.

Carla hung up her receiver in time to see a small cousin teetering on a drainboard in an effort to reach the cookie jar. She rushed in, whisked the girl off and gave her a cookie. Within moments, three more were in the kitchen yapping around like puppies demanding equal treatment. While appeasing them all, she threw a wistful look at the kitchen clock to see how long it would be before cousin Daisy got back from work. Yelling and laughing, the others surged into the living room, and Carla slipped into the small backyard.

Chasing the dog out of the vegetable patch, she threw herself into weeding. Around here, she discovered, work usually guaranteed solitude.

It was good to hear from Dan, but he certainly sounded strange. What could be such a big secret he couldn't talk about it on the phone? Did the FBI bug candidates' phones? Weird.

Well, anyway, it would get her out of the house tomorrow. She hadn't been looking forward to Saturday with no Smithsonian classes. She was enjoying the classes; they made her heritage seem a proud thing, not the embarrassment her mother seemed to find it. But this summer, classes were particularly welcome as an escape from this dingy house full of kids and pets.

She yanked spindly weeds from around the tomatoes while making up fantasic suggestions for Dan's big secret.

That evening at home, Dan only picked at his dinner. When his mother objected, he said he must have eaten too much pizza at lunch. Not a very convincing lie, he realized; he could never eat too much pizza.

Before going to bed, he removed the envelope from under the teddy bear, tore it up, burned the shreds in the sink, and flushed the ashes down the toilet. He went to bed feeling cold and calm. He wondered if he was in shock.

Next morning, he got to the rendezvous half an hour early. The day was beginning to be hot and muggy. Already his tee shirt was sticking to him, and he wished he'd worn shorts instead of jeans. The summer tourists were out in force, but they never seemed as bad here as at other "national shrines." Maybe that's why he liked the Jefferson Memorial best.

And it was definitely the sort of place for this meeting. All the spy stories say that public places are the most private. Suddenly he looked around him, wondering how many of the people lounging about, strolling or talking quietly in pairs were really spies. Maybe they all were. Not a legitimate tourist among them. He laughed at himself and felt, if not less nervous, at least less conspicuous.

Mechanically, he paced about the monument, its huge circle of marble pillars looking like the top layer of a gigantic wedding cake. Over and over again in his mind, he rehearsed what he would say. He was so absorbed, he didn't notice Carla until she planted herself firmly in his path. "Hi, remember me?"

"Oh!" He jumped. "Yes, thanks for coming. Let's go somewhere with fewer people." Before she could say anything, he trotted down the stairs, leading her to the broad path that ran along the sparkling waters of the Tidal Basin. The way was lined with cherry trees, looking in midsummer like ordinary green trees and not the blossomy confections that draw the spring camera buffs.

"Well," Carla said after they'd walked some distance in silence, "aren't you going to ask me to marry you?"

"Marry you?" He spun around.

"Isn't that what young men always mean when they tell a girl they have something important to say to them?"

He blushed.

"But, I'm afraid the answer is no," she continued playfully. "I don't want to live in the White House. Too big and gloomy."

"Well, actually . . ."

"Actually what? Come on, Dan, you've worked yourself into a stew. Now just sit on this bench and *tell* me something."

They sat down, and before his mind froze up, Dan threw away all his mental scripts and jumped into it.

"Carla, suppose I told you that if that top secret project your mom's working on succeeds, a bunch of really weird creatures from outer space are going to rush in and make Earth a colony, and it will mean the end of human independence and culture?"

Several expressions flowed over Carla's face, settling into a thoughtful frown. "Well, I'd probably say the experiment should fail, and Mom ought to look for another job."

"Then you'll help me?"

"Help you write your book? That's what you're doing, isn't it? Writing a science fiction story?"

"Boy, I wish I were. No, let me explain."

For an hour he did.

At the end, Carla stood up. "That's heavy stuff, you know. Let's walk some more." They got up and strolled along the waterside path, avoiding clumps of picture-taking tourists.

"Suppose I believe you (and you shouldn't, but just suppose) then would it really be so bad? I mean we don't know what kind of colonizers they'd be. And we'd be instantly part of all that fantastic stuff: space, travel, galactic empires, and all."

Dan scowled in frustration, trying to remember how Greer had put things. He remembered his own words instead.

"I don't think it matters how kind the colonists are or what they offer. You have your own people as an example: the American Indians. The settlers came in and destroyed them, not just with bullets but with their way of life. You've said it yourself. Your people have bought that flashy American lifestyle—the cars and TVs and all that. And they've lost almost everything of their own. You're studying it now; think what they could have given: not just the pots and blankets, but stuff like the oneness of things and closeness to the land. All that."

Carla nodded. "Yeah, the comparison's hit me, too. I'm not saying I agree to help you, or even believe you. But let's go see that funny friend of yours."

"He's not very funny now, except for the eyes. I guess he uses a whole lot of depilatory or somethng."

They both laughed. Dan felt a tightness loosen inside. It was a lot better not being alone in this.

Several hours later, in Greer's apartment, Dan watched Carla go through the same shock and disbelief that he had. With the station's inhabitants, she too seemed torn between interest and repulsion.

The third research student had made an appearance, and Dan would as soon it hadn't. It resembled a large gelatin pancake. It moved around on an extruded carpet of oil bubbles, which, fortunately for the housekeeping, it seemed to reabsorb as it passed. It was interesting enough, but the thing's extreme alienness made Dan uneasy, particularly when it talked.

But what Carla seemed to find even more intriguing, and what perhaps did the most to convince her, were the maps Greer showed them. They were actually orbital photographs of the area around the research project. Printed on sheets of odd oily-feeling paper, they were perfectly three dimensional.

Looking at them, one had the feeling of peering over an impossibly high precipice into the real world. It made Dan's stomach tighten. He had to clutch the edge of the table while he looked at them. With relief he noticed that Carla also hung back.

Not only were the photos in perfect three dimension, they were wonderfully detailed. Each tree, rock and blade of grass stood out. Dan was sure that if he looked closely enough, he'd see ants marching over the rocks.

Having reluctantly accepted the truth of Greer's story, Carla admitted there seemed only one conclusion. "My grandmother used to say that when people abandon their own ways, they lose their souls, too. No matter what they wear or do after that, they are dead people, and so are their children and their children's children. It used to frighten me. My mother said she was crazy, but I don't think she was." She was silent a moment, then looked at Greer. "What can I do to help?"

He smiled gratefully. "What I really need is someone on the inside, not to fiddle with the machinery, but to learn what they can about the installation."

Carla swallowed hard, imagining herself sneaking around her mother's lab, jotting treasonous notes. She didn't like the picture. "You know, no one's going to tell a dumb kid very much," she said, hoping he'd decide the idea was a dud.

"No, actually I think people tend to run off at the mouth with children. They think they can brag without their audience knowing enough to criticize.

But don't worry, you won't have to memorize anything or even takes notes. You'll have a camera and can photograph everything in sight. I can learn what I need from that."

She closed her eyes. She'd have to do it—there didn't seem any other choice. But she still felt queasy. "I suppose that sounds easy enough," she said after a moment. "And my mom would probably be happy to have me visit. But she knows I haven't the money to just flit out there on impulse."

"Money's no problem," Greer said casually. "I make my own."

Dan's mouth fell open. "I thought you were living a little high on the hog up here."

Greer smiled. "I couldn't afford this place on what your dad pays me, that's for certain. No, I brought a matter replicator down with me. It's just a small one, but it does fine for money and such."

"And my dad said anthropology doesn't pay," Dan muttered.

"Well, it's great that *you* have money," Carla said to Greer. "But we still need a story to explain how penniless Carla is able to suddenly take off for Nevada."

"Maybe we could say it was a field trip connected with your Smithsonian course," Dan suggested. "You're such a whiz, they are covering your expenses . . ."

"Good," she said thoughtfully, "A field trip to

study petroglyphs. There're a lot of Indian rock drawings in Nevada."

"Perhaps," Greer added, "we could use the same cover for you, Dan. I may need your help as well, if your willing to come along."

"Oh, I wouldn't miss this," Dan said more boldly than he felt. "It'll be a great break from fund-raising dinners and hearing Dad's speech for the five hundredth time. But how do we work it out with my folks? Our lives are pretty tightly scheduled, you know."

"That'll be easy enough," Greer replied. "You're going to Senator Karstell's ranch in Idaho next week. Tell your parents that you and I are going off for a few days to look at petroglyph sites. They know you're keen on archaeology, and you can tell them petroglyphs are a special hobby of mine."

Dan looked doubtful. "Doesn't that sound a little fishy? I mean, you and I haven't exactly been close buddies all these years."

Greer grinned. "Tell them you got to know me better at the convention and learned the important moral lesson that people are not always what they seem."

Dan snorted. Corny. Very corny. But true.

Chapter 8

The sun was at its zenith. Beneath it, the landscape lay unmercifully hot. Two mountain ranges stretched for miles, bare and rocky under its blaze. Between, spread a wide valley, one of many in this dry country; a valley of gray-green sagebrush, white dust and dry, crinkly grass.

Nothing moved in the shimmer of midday heat. Time itself seemed to have stopped. The insects were stilled, the lizards dozed in cool rock shadows. All life waited for the sun to move on, for the mountains to take on shape again, to cast their reviving purple shadows across the valley floor.

In this negation of life, something moved. In protest, a pale cloud of dust twisted and rose up into the windless air. On a dirt road, cutting like a scar across the valley, a determined brown van was moving, spewing up dust in a bold, dry wake.

The person at the wheel enjoyed the heat. It soaked into him like a memory of home. But the glaring light was harsh and alien. Even through dark glasses, he strained to see the road and keep their jolting, dust-whitening vehicle on the narrow course.

Beside him Dan Stratton sat slouched down, his head bouncing against the back of the seat. The heat was stupefying, but he couldn't sleep for the constant jolting—and the worry. This wasn't a story, and it it wasn't a fantasy about what he'd do someday. He had made a decision, a real one. And he hoped it was the right one, because the actions that were following were very real. He had that awful hollow feeling you get a split second after leaving a diving board. He'd committed himself to something big, and he wasn't sure he liked it.

But at the moment, even the worry and tension were beaten into the background by the heat. It seemed all he could do was to endure and stare ahead at the very non-midwestern landscape. All color had been drained from the scene, and it was oddly flat, like a theatrical backdrop. The approaching mountains had lost all distance and depth.

Next to him, Carla Brenner sat dangling an arm out the open window. The searing wind of their passage flapped at her shirt, snatching up the sweat before it could dampen the fabric. The only sound in the world was that flapping shirt and the steady rumbling of the van.

The wind rasped at her dark hair. Mechanically she pushed it back, and for an instant the sun glinted off the silver and turquoise of her bracelet. The sight slipped into her troubled thoughts.

Years ago, her grandmother had given her that bracelet, an heirloom old even to her. Too big for Carla that day on the reservation, it fit her well now, looking rich and ancient against her brown skin. She'd worn it to remind her, to call her back if she drifted into doubt. She had a task to do for her grandmother, and maybe for her grandchildren. But she needed support, the bracelet if nothing else. She was afraid.

They were clearly closer to the mountains now. One spur had peeled itself off from the flatness and was jutting out at them on the left. Farther on, another rib of mountain appeared, sticking into the valley on their right. The dirt road, unsigned as it had been for its whole length, ran between the two and curved sharply to the north.

A new view opened up, a small pocket valley protected by two arms of the mountains. In the distance still, back where the rocky mountainside rose from the valley floor, a series of low buildings splashed a line of unnatural white and sun-reflecting metal across their view.

Slowly the van drew near the structures. To the south, clustered half a dozen low buildings, featureless except for occasional dark windows. North of these, stretching for at least a mile across the valley floor, glinted a structure of corrugated metal, looking like half a giant sewer pipe. The whole complex was enclosed by a high cyclone fence.

As the van rumbled toward the gate, Dan slumped further down in the seat and pulled the cap down over his eyes.

"Relax," Carla said. "Nobody's going to know who you are. To adults, all kids look alike"

"Yeah. But *I* know who I am, and that's scary enough."

Greer stopped the van well outside the gate with its sentry box and armed guard. He looked over at Carla and tried a reassuring smile. "Well, we've done all the rehearsing we can. What's the term in theater? Break a leg?"

She opened the van door, grabbing up her rucksack from the floor of the cab, and hopped out. "Yeah, thanks . . . I think."

The door slammed with metalic finality. Theater was the right analogy, she thought. Enter the adventurous young heroine. Jane Bond off to save the world.

After a few feet she turned back, waved and called loudly, "Thanks, Professor. Hope you and the other students have a good time in Reno. See you Wednesday."

Shouldering her pack, she marched resolutely toward the gate. The soldier stepped out, and she threw him an innocently confident smile.

"Hi, I'm Carla Brenner, come to visit my mother, Maria Brenner . . . Dr. Maria Brenner."

The young soldier consulted a clipboard in his hand. "No one here by that name," he said after a minute. "Try another."

"Huh?" She frowned in confusion. "Oh, maybe she's using her maiden name. Maria Fallencloud?"

He looked at her evenly. "We do have one of those, and she's expecting a guest."

Bureaucratic twerp, Carla thought. "Thanks. May I go in?"

Checking off a spot on his clipboard, the other nodded brusquely. Carla took a few steps through the gate and waved at the van. Immediately the engine roared to life, and in a minute it was only a receding cloud of dust. She felt very alone.

Automatically, her hand went to her bracelet and then to her ring. The ring came not from her grandmother, but from David Greer, or whatever his real name was—he'd told them they couldn't pronounce it. Impossibly, the ring concealed a camera, activated by squeezing her fingers. Jane Bond, indeed!

Resolutely she trudged through the heat toward the low clustered buildings. A small dark figure was hurrying toward her, and suddenly she was happy. Spy or not, she needed a familiar, loving face. She ran toward her mother.

They hugged each other, fighting back happy tears. Carla realized she needn't have felt guilty about this pretext for a visit. She really did miss her mom. Maybe they could be together more after this.

Chattering happily, they walked back toward the compound. "So, how is this field trip going?"

"Oh, great," Carla lied, then quickly followed with a truth. "I'm really learning a lot."

Suddenly remembering her strategy, she added, "But I do get a little tired of all those dead Indians. I want to see what a live Indian is doing for a change. I want a complete red-carpet tour of this place, and learned explanations of all the important stuff you're doing. Pretend I'm a visiting VIP who gives out grant money or something."

Her mother laughed. "Oh, we can't do that, we haven't dusted everything! Not that it would make any difference with all the dust around this dump. But I'll give you the non-grant-givers tour."

She led Carla into one of the neat white buildings, introducing her to co-workers they passed in the halls, and then showed her their room.

A small tidy room, it was crowded now with an extra cot. One antiseptic white wall was splashed with color, the bright red, blue and yellow of an Indian rug. Carla felt a jab of happiness. First her old name, and now this. Her mother, too, was trying to hold on.

After she'd washed and told all the news about her brother, sister and cousins, Carla started her tour. They began with the lab where her mother did most of her work. Somewhat guiltily at first, Carla squeezed her ring at everything.

In another lab, she was introduced to Paul Bloom, a heavy man with a sweaty face and a laugh like bubbling oatmeal. No, Carla decided, not heavy. He was just plain fat, particularly in a white lab coat. She could tell by the tone in her mother's voice that this was her current boyfriend and that she wasn't particularly proud of it. On the wall by his desk was a poster from the movie *Love on a Far Star*. The heroine, clad only in metal bikini and space helmet, was firing two ray guns at a many armed green guy with a lecherous leer.

Carla decided she did not like Paul Bloom. Chalk up a less cosmic reason for getting her mom out of this.

Dinner in the mess hall surprised Carla. Obviously, she thought as she savored the chicken in wine sauce, all of President Wainwright's secret money had not been spent on silicon chips and wires.

Afterwards, at Carla's suggestion, her mother showed her around the administrative wing. They ran into Dr. Svengard bustling down the hall. He acknowledged them with a curt nod, and Carla thought that he still seemed like an arrogant jerk. But her attention was fixed on the room he'd come out of. Bold black letters spelled "Facilities Office" across the paneling.

"What's that?" she asked innocently.

"Oh, that's where they run this place from, and

store all the plans for the building and security systems, I guess. Now the library is down here. Just technical journals and reference books mostly."

Carla scarcely listened, her mind firmly on the last room.

Next morning her mother had to work, and Carla said not to worry, she'd amuse herself and keep out of people's way. For a while she walked around the buildings aimlessly, pointing her ring at whatever looked important. Then she strolled outside.

The fence, some distance from the buildings, enclosed a very large chunk of valley floor. Casually she walked toward it, all the while searching the ground as if for arrowheads. After a time, she stopped in surprise. She'd actually found one.

Reaching down almost reverently, she picked up the gray leaf-shaped flint, its edge rippled with tiny flakes. A beautiful thing, she thought, and something all ours—part of what makes humans human. She closed her hand on the sun-warmed stone. It pressed against her palm like an ancient promise.

"Better not go much further," a voice said behind her. Startled, she spun around. A guard, a different one thankfully, was walking toward her.

"I'm just looking for artifacts, arrowheads and things. See, I found one!"

"Sure, that's okay. It's just those poles. You want to watch out for them."

He pointed to a tall metal pole some twenty feet from her, standing between her and the distant fence.

"I really don't think I'd trip over it," she said.

"No, but you might trip it, so to speak." The young man laughed at his own joke. "It's part of the inner security screen, you see."

"Oh," she said, suddenly interested. "How does it work?"

"Well, that outer fence, see, it keeps out casual intruders. Not that we have many out here except for the occasional coyote or antelope. If anything big get past that, it probably did it deliberately. But when it walks between those poles—see, there's a whole line of them—it breaks the current and sets off an intruder alarm in one of the buildings."

"My, that's ingenious," she said waving a be-ringed hand at what she now saw was a line of free-standing poles marching off in both directions. "But what if a rabbit or something squeezes through the outer fence? You might have a lot of false alarms."

"No, whatever current passes between those poles gives off some sort of vibrations that little animals don't like. But people don't notice it."

"Wow, that's like out of some science fiction movie."

"Yeah," he agreed. "This whole place is."

Carla thanked him for his warning and promised to stay clear of the poles. As she continued strolling, gradually inching closer for a better picture, she thought about the guard's science fiction movie. She wondered which plot it was. The secret desert laboratory accidentally producing giant cockroaches that take over the world? How about the winged guy from outer space who wants to blow up the President's secret space experiment? The first sounded more believable.

That afternoon, Carla got her mother to show her the impressively long quonset hut that dominated the complex. Walking through the doorway, they casually passed the "Authorized Personnel Only" sign. The domed metal shed, some one hundred feet across, was lit by glaring worklights, which disappeared into the distance. Down its center, for apparently its whole length, stretched a cluster of shiny metal pipes, supported at intervals by pillars, with a maze of wires and tubes at the bases.

The nearest pillar, where the pipes ended, was larger than the rest. Two lab-coated technicians were adjusting something near the transparent sphere at the top, while a third was on his belly using a small blowtorch on the base.

"This is where it's all eventually supposed to happen," Carla's mother said. "Wish I could tell you exactly what, but it's still supposed to be a secret."

Carla, looking politely interested, edged closer to the terminal pillar, hand slightly outstretched. "Do you think it'll work, whatever it is?"

Her mother lowered her voice. "Well, most academics think Svengard's a crank. But if his theory is correct, everything else should follow. And if it isn't —well, at least I'll get out of this desert prison camp."

That night, Carla lay in her bed, tense and unsleeping. She was leaving tomorrow, and though she'd seen most of what she could, there was still one goal that had eluded her. Patience, she told herself.

Rolling on her side, she looked out the moon-whitened patch of window. In the distance, a coyote howled. She wondered if the others in the van somewhere could hear it, too. What a pair they were; and she liked them both. Dan, of course, was just plain likable, to her anyway. But she even liked David Greer, particularly when he kept his glasses on.

Inside the bed-crowded room, the sound of her mother's fitful tossing sank into slow steady breathing. Carla waited until the moon, slightly past full, had completed its cross of her window. Then, with the room in darkness again, she swung her feet out of bed and pulled on a jacket.

With questing fingers, she checked the inner pocket. The device Greer had given her was still there. As small as a hairpin, it even looked like one, with what seemed to be a special decorative knob at one end.

She stood for a moment, listening to her mother's steady breathing, then slipped quietly out the door. The hallway was lit by dim, widely-spaced bulbs. With a racing heart, she sped barefoot along it, hoping she could remember all the correct turns. If she met anyone, she'd say she got lost looking for the bathroom.

There were still lights and voices behind a few of the doors, but no one came into the hall. She reached the "Facilities Office" almost before she knew it. She tried the knob. Locked. Swiftly, she drew the pin from her pocket and jammed it into the keyhole. Twisting the bulb, she heard a tiny click. The doorknob turned easily. Dropping the pin back into her pocket, she stepped inside.

Standing inside the closed door, she let her beating heart get back to normal. The room was dark, and she cursed herself for not bringing a flashlight. She'd have to switch on the light and hope that no one would see.

She did so and saw a small room less bare than the others, not from fancy decor, but because desks, file cabinets and tables were everywhere. With a resigned sigh, she began opening drawers and squeezing her ring at every piece of paper that looked useful.

By the time she'd reached the last drawer, the adrenaline had drained away, leaving her tired and jumpy. This file looked useless, correspondence mostly. She began flipping through the next when suddenly the door behind her opened. The dumpling face of Paul Bloom peered in, eyes wide with surprise.

"Well, well, a pretty little burglar in our midst," he said with an oily bubble.

"Oh!" She spun around. "You startled me!"

"I was supposed to. This room's off limits, you know."

"Is it?" she said with wide-eyed innocence. "The door wasn't locked."

"It should have been."

"Well, it wasn't. The library's closed, and I was looking for someplace with maps of the area. I thought that if Mom had to work tomorrow morning, I'd spend the time looking for petroglyph sites—Indian rock drawings, you know."

She didn't like the supercilious smile on the fat lips. She liked being in this little room with him even less and wished she was wearing more than just a nightgown and jacket. Moving quickly to the door, she jerked it open and stepped into the hall. His grab for her fell short. He followed her out.

"If they're so private about this place," she said indignantly as she moved hastily away, "tell them to lock the door."

"Forget about maps, sweetie," he said to her retreating back. "Spend the morning in the libary reading Oz books or whatever it is little girls like."

Little girls! She wondered if Greer knew any voracious alien monsters to feed this slimeball to.

Chapter 9

At two the next afternoon, Carla and her mother walked to the gate. A dusty brown van was parked some distance beyond it. Carla could see the "professor" at the wheel and guessed that his eager young student was scrunched down on the seat beside him.

Carla turned to her mother. "How long are you going to be here, Mom? Cousin Daisy's nice, but we all miss you."

The woman sighed. "I know. I'd like to be home, too. I guess it depends on how the experiment two weeks from now goes. If it fizzles—good thing old Svengard didn't hear that—but if it does, I'll probably be packing my bags right afterwards. If it succeeds, who knows?"

They hugged in farewell, and grabbing up her

bag, Carla trotted out to the waiting van. She hopped into the cab, waving to her mother as they drove off.

The three in the van said little to each other until they were well away from the complex, as if the very sagebrush might be bugged. Finally, Dan broke the silence. "Well, Secret Agent Carla, how did it go?"

She sighed and leaned back against the seat. "Pretty well, I guess, but I still don't know which sort of spy I should feel like, James Bond or Benedict Arnold."

"Bond," Dan replied. "Arnold worked for the bad guys."

She looked at him. "And that's the difference between a patriot and a traitor?"

"What else?"

She laughed. "Okay, as a patriot, loyal to humanity, I 'ringed' everything in sight and would have ended up in the brig last night if I hadn't been such a quick liar. But what have you two been up to while I've been doing all the dirty work?"

"Oh, we've been getting into our share of dirt," Greer said. "Wouldn't you say so, Dan?"

The boy grinned. "Yeah. This supposedly four-wheel drive vehicle got stuck in a dry streambed, and we spent hours digging it out."

"As for the rest of the time," Greer said, "we were—what's the term—casing the joint? Checking out the best routes into the mountains, finding the best vantage points, and so forth."

"We even found some real petroglyphs!" Dan

added, "to ease our consciences. And one wasn't even in the guide. Here, let me show you." He rummaged through the glove compartment for an already tattered guidebook. The two spent a while poring over the maps and drawings while the small, thin man in the dark glasses guided the van along the rough road.

Eventually their dirt track joined a paved highway, and they turned east following it back through the mountains well to the north of where they had just been. From the summit of the pass, other purple mountain ranges could be seen in both directions, with sage-filled valleys dipping between them and their own range. Highway traffic was limited to a few dark specks inching along the ribbons of road that laid civilization's light claim on this landscape.

At the bottom of the pass, they turned off onto another dirt road and jogged along for several more miles before leaving the track altogether and jolting off into the rapidly rising mountains.

After a long bone-shaking while, Greer pulled the van behind a screen of piñon pines and turned off the motor. Following hours of steady rumbling, the silence fell heavily around them.

The sun had left the east face of these mountains hours earlier, but across the basin, it cast a rosy sunset glow on the next range of peaks. They stepped out into the chill dusk as a few insects tentatively chirped into the slowly healing silence.

Already into the camping routine, Dan brought out the campstove and began opening cans of beans and Spam. Greer took Carla's ring into the back of the van to prepare the pictures it had taken.

As they finished a desert of canned peaches and cookies, he complimented her on her thoroughness. "There's a lot of useful material there," he concluded, "particularly about the security system. Too bad you couldn't get any detailed circuitry plans of the device itself, but the actual pictures of it are good. I think I know what to do now."

"Are you familiar with how these things are put together?" Dan asked.

"The principle is basic, but different species apply it differently. I'm no physicist, but this is a pretty primitive device. I think I can handle it."

A thought suddenly jabbed Carla like a hot knife. "You're not going to make it explode, are you? Will those people down there be hurt?"

"No, they'll be safe. The information you brought back shows they all plan to observe the test from an installation some distance away. Of course, I'd like to make the failure as dramatic and convincing as possible, and a nice nuclear explosion would do that. But that might also give them the idea they were on to a new weapon, and they'd triple the research effort. So I've decided on an implosion, something that collapses the machinery and buildings in on themselves—in a modest way."

Dark had closed in completely when Greer hauled the sleeping bags from the back of the van. Dan and Carla unrolled theirs on the needle-softened ground beneath the scraggly pines, but Greer chose a large sagebrush, stomped it somewhat flat, and dumped his bag on top of it.

Noticing the others' incredulous stares, he said, "At least out here I can design my own furniture. One of the hardest things these last few years has been trying to look comfortable in yours."

Crawling into the bag in its sagebrush nest, he curled up like a cat. The others stretched out, listening to the comfortingly earthly sounds of wind in the pines, and tried to think restful thoughts.

Next morning Greer woke them while the trees overhead were still dark silhouettes against predawn gray. The air was cold outside their sleeping bags, and they quickly hopped into the back of the van to eat a hurried breakfast and ready their packs for the journey ahead.

Greer helped the two young people into backpacks, but for himself only buckled a small beltpack and canteen about his waist. "Sorry to make you carry so much of the burden, but our bodies simply aren't designed to carry weight on our backs. From our waists, yes, but your packs don't work that way."

Before putting them away, Greer unrolled one of the three-dimensional photos. Again it seemed more than a photo, a magically captured segment of reality. The two humans hung slightly back from the illusion of height while Greer traced one thin finger along their proposed route.

"We'll go this way, I think. It's not the most direct route, but considering our varied abilities . . ." He grinned at Dan. "It's probably the best."

Carla bristled. "Now wait a minute. If that's some sort of sexist slur . . ."

"It's not sexist," Dan assured her, "just speciesist. Remember, I've been with this character for three days now."

Greer cuffed Dan playfully on the head. Packing away the photos, he said, "My ancestors evolved scaling cliffs, not running across plains after zebra. Terrain like this is my specialty. On the other hand, I wouldn't challenge either of you to a footrace."

Amber sunrise had just touched the peaks above them as they started out. After a short while Greer sat down on a boulder and removed his shoes.

"Here comes old spider toes," Dan remarked.

"Give a guy a break," Greer complained. "We're not likely to meet anyone out here, and wearing these shoes is like walking with bricks on my feet."

He yanked off the last sock, and with a satisfied sigh wiggled the four long toes of each foot. The morning sun glinted off dark claws.

Carla stared at them, then glanced quickly at his hands. Greer smiled. "Yes, I used to have lovely hands like that too, until I had them altered for this assignment. It didn't help my handwriting any." He jumped up, feet clutching the ground like living creatures. "Come on, let's get going."

He scrambled on ahead, though never so far that

the others lost sight of him or their route. What they followed was no discernible path, but a roughly linked chain of scrub-filled ravines, rocky slopes and dry streambeds. Steadily they cut deeper and higher into the mountains.

Steadily, too, the sun grew hotter. The shadows shortened, becoming sharp-edged and black against the glaring rock. The air seemed to shimmer, blurring the landscape around them. The only life they saw was a startled rabbit, an occasional scurrying lizard, and distant specks of hawks circling in the blue sky.

Choking with the smell of hot dust and their own sweat, Dan and Carla took more and more frequent sips from their canteens. But they shared an unspoken consent not to let the honor of their species down and kept plugging ahead although their legs and feet screamed at them for a rest.

After hours of this, Carla stumbled mechanically around a boulder and stopped abruptly at the sight of Greer crouching like a skinny frog on a shadowed ledge.

"Break time," he announced cheerfully.

Dan staggered up behind her, squinting at his surroundings as though suddenly coming awake. "Oh, yeah, I remember this place. Petroglyphs. I'll show you, Carla, if I ever catch my breath."

"Food first," Greer said, rummaging around in the pack that Carla had gratefully shrugged off. They shared a meal of dates, beef jerky, plums and granola bars, along with sips from the canteens.

Halfway through, Carla asked, "Can you eat all our food? You don't have your friends parachute down special supplies?"

Greer licked the sticky plum juice off his fingers. "If I pick and choose, I can manage. In theory our requirements are similar, but I had some pretty rough times at first before I learned what I could take and what I couldn't. Fortunately I did bring along plenty of stomach remedies."

As they finished, Dan pulled the guidebook out of his pack. He turned to one of the maps. "See, the site marked here is just around that rock. And this "x" is the site we found up the hillside there. We may have been the first ever to find it!"

"Well, let me look at the close one," Carla said. "After a week supposedly studying petroglyphs, I ought to see at least one."

Dan led her to where an overhanging rock was partially hidden by spidery manzanita. Pushing branches aside, they saw that the rock surface was daubed with patches of red-orange paint, which, as they looked, gradually resolved into distinct shapes: triangles, spirals and ladder marks, and some that might be people or animals.

After a while Carla said. "Exciting—but frustrating, too. People really have no idea what they mean?"

"Nothing but guesses," Greer said. "They're old. But it's not just that the people who made them are dead. Their whole culture is dead. Whatever these could have told us is lost."

He extended a hand toward the rock surface, and Carla saw he was wearing the camera ring. He smiled at her. "I'm still an anthropologist at heart, you know, not a political saboteur."

"And you're especially fond of dead cultures," Dan added dryly.

"Cheer up. Yours isn't dead yet."

They started out again. As the day crept into afternoon, they cut their way higher into the mountains. A dry breeze snapped at their hair and clothing, carrying the warm scent of sage and dust and piñon pine. As they climbed, a purple range of mountains appeared in the distance. White billowing thunderheads piled above it, innocent and silent at this distance. Above their own mountains, the sky arched a sharp, clear blue.

The shadows had lengthened and the sun hung as a swollen orange globe over the western mountains, when Greer finally called a halt. Dropping their packs in front of a shallow cave, they walked cautiously across a bare dome of rock. As they neared the drop-off, Greer got down on hands and knees and, motioning the others to do the same, scuttled to the edge.

Beyond them stretched a dry basin misted with sage, its far side already sunk in evening shadow. Directly below, in the small side valley, a cluster of low white buildings glowed warmly in the setting sun.

Dan brought the binoculars from his pack, and after scanning the view for a minute, handed them to Carla. She studied the buildings, their familiarity oddly distorted by the strange angle. At first she hoped to see her mother, but then decided the more impersonal she kept this, the better.

She passed the glasses on to Greer, but he shook his head. "My distance vision's all right, thanks. But let's stay back from the edge until dark."

At the mouth of their cave, they ate a cold supper. Chewing dryly on his peanut butter sandwich, Dan leaned back against a slab of stone, its rough surface giving back the day's soaked-in warmth. Across the valley a crimson sun slid behind the dark peaks. Around them, the rock took on a brief rosy glow before purple dusk swept over them and on to the peaks above.

"Well, David," he said, biting into a tart apple, "what's the plan of attack?"

Greer chucked his own apple core and watched it bounce over the bare rock and into a rustling bush. "After all our scouting, it still seems this is the best launch point for me and the best vantage point for you. But Carla's route will be a bit tricky. I'd better get the photos."

"I still think I should be the one to go down there," Dan protested. "I was the one who dragged Carla into this. I shouldn't sit back and let her take all the risks."

"Maybe you should both let me in on this discussion," Carla suggested.

116

"The problem," Greer said, removing his glasses now that the offensive sunlight was gone, "is that I can't do this alone. The atmosphere is thinner and the gravity greater than at home. Even from this height, it's going to be hard for me to keep airborne long enough to get inside the defenses, particularly since I'm rather out of shape after all these grounded years."

"You're going to fly down there?" Carla asked incredulously.

He nodded. "I should just be able to make it. But your photos showed I'll need some relatively heavy materials. If I carry them myself, it may be too much drag, so I need someone to bring them by surface. Once I'm beyond that row of security poles, I can deactivate them long enough to let you pass."

Dan objected. "I still think I should . . ."

"We can't risk it. There's too much chance of something going wrong. If Carla is caught, it would be hard on her personally, but she could probably bluff enough to keep off outside investigation. But if you're caught, Dan, they'd find out who you are, and that would finish your father. They needn't bother with an election. 'Son of Anti-Space Candidate Tries to Sabotage Secret Space Project'—the ultimate political dirty trick."

Dan was quiet a moment. "But what if you're caught?"

"Then the game's really up. I imagine colonization orders would go through immediately. I could only hope that before the others arrived, the police wouldn't send me to a zoo or start dissecting me."

After a silence, Greer continued. "And to reduce the chances of all that happening, we need someone up here. I have a pair of night binoculars for you and a set of walkie-talkies, lifted from the convention supplies. You'll have a fine overview of what's happening down there and can report if anyone comes near us. I also have a weapon for you."

He reached into a pocket and brought out a metallic disk two inches across. Alarmed, Dan said, "Why should I need a weapon?"

"I don't know, you probably won't. We have no reason to believe there are any security patrols up here. They wouldn't expect this sort of approach. But there are wild animals about, and you'll be alone up here for a long while. We all should be armed. I have one for Carla, too."

"How does it work?" Dan asked, eyeing the object in his hand as if it were a coiled serpent. A grill marked one end of the disk. Otherwise it was featureless except for a smaller raised disk in the center.

"Well, it isn't designed for your hands, or mine anymore. But you aim this opening at your target, like this. Good. Then . . . let me adjust the setting here, we needn't be too violent. Then you slide this catch back. Careful where you point it! That's better. Aim at one of those little rocks over there, and when you're ready, press the center."

118

Dan squinted at the rocks through the deepening dusk, trying to line them up with the grid opening. Placing a thumb on the center disk, he pressed.

What shot out was not so much a beam of light as a rippling in the air, a bubbling disturbance as if something had been dropped through water. One of the rocks (not quite the one he had aimed for) swelled with a brief golden glow and burst into dust.

Dan wanted to drop the thing and stomp on it. Instead he stood frozen, staring at the disk. "My God!"

"It's nice and portable," Greer said matter-of-factly. "Not too powerful, but a good personal weapon. I doubt if either of you will need it."

"I should hope not," Carla whispered, accepting her own disk with considerable reluctance.

"We won't launch this effort for a while yet," Greer said. "But you'll have to start down before I do, Carla. It's really a fairly easy route, and I've a light that's not detectable from a distance. Let's go over the route."

By flashlight glow, they traced the descent on the three-D photos. Once she felt confident she could find the way, they crept to the cliff's edge and watched the lights twinkling below, a small, lonely cluster in a great darkness.

A refrain floated into Dan's mind, "the hopes and fears of all the years are met in thee tonight." He shivered. The responsibility was more than he could grasp—or wanted.

At one point in the night, twin headlights moved

out of the gate and jolted off along the main dirt road. "Probably heading to the bright lights of Austin, Nevada," Carla said. "My mom says it's right out of a western movie, mahogany bar and all. The staff sometimes go there on weekends, but off-duty guards go almost every night."

After a time, they rolled over and looked upwards. Dan sighed. "I keep forgetting how spectacular mountain nights are. We used to go camping in Colorado. There are so many stars."

"They are beautiful," Carla said after a while. "But they look so cold and lonely."

"Not if they're home," Greer said quietly.

Carla rolled over and looked at him, his curled up figure a darker lump in the darkness. "I bet this has all been pretty lonely for you."

A soft sound that could have been a sigh. "It would have been easier if I'd felt free to mingle with you people. Mine is a very sociable species; we're not fond of isolation. And I've been away from home seventeen years now."

"And you're still a graduate student?" Dan asked jokingly, then he sobered. "How old are you anyway?"

"Oh, about seventy-three of your years." To their gasps, he replied, "In actual terms, I'm not much older than you are—a kid fresh out of college so to speak. Our life spans are longer, but the extra isn't tacked on uselessly at the end. The whole thing is just stretched out."

"Can you see your home from here?" Carla asked after a moment.

"No, not really. It's deep into the galaxy off that way." He pointed to where the arching brilliance of the Milky Way dropped toward the southern horizon. "The anthropology institute where I studied is closer though. You can't actually see its sun, but it's up there beyond that lower star in Cygnus the Swan."

They were silent a while, contemplating the glitter overhead. On a ledge below them, a night bird called, then flew darkly between them and the stars.

Greer stood up. "It's time for you to get ready, Carla. The moon will be up soon and that ought to help you."

Back at the cave, Greer reorganized one of the packs so it held only what would be needed that night. As Carla slipped it on her back, he handed her the dark flashlight and a rolled photo of her route. To her belt she clipped one of the walkie-talkies.

They all walked to where the rock outcrop dropped into a deep ravine. "I'm not even going to suggest you break a leg this time," Greer said. "Call in every few minutes and let us know how you're doing."

Dan felt awkward. He didn't know whether to shake hands or hug her. He did neither. "Be careful, Carla. I wish you didn't have to—"

"Hey, man, don't go all heroic on me." She glanced down at the dull gleam of her bracelet. "This is my world too, you know."

As she descended into the scrub-filled ravine, the waning moon broke free of the jagged peaks above. Instantly the landscape was splotched with contrasts: silvery white and deep black shadows.

Dan and Greer watched Carla disappear from sight, then returned to the edge of the cliff. Several minutes later the walkie-talkie squawked into life. "This is Strike Leader, just checking in."

Greer spoke into the receiver. "How's it going?"

"Fine. This is faster then I thought. Gravity helps, I guess. A moment ago, something furry darted across my path. Don't know who was more afraid. But I'm breathing again."

"Good. Take care, and keep checking in. How's one supposed to say it? Over and out?"

"Roger."

Greer looked perplexed as he put the device down. "My name's not Roger."

"A quaint local saying." Dan laughed.

They followed Carla's progress first by her reports then by actually watching as she flitted from shadow to shadow across the valley floor. When she reached the outer cyclone fence, she called in.

"Okay, climb over it," Greer instructed. "There's a tree this side of the poles. Head toward that and wait there. But *don't go closer*. I'll be with you in a few minutes.

He stood up and started getting undressed. "I should have done this earlier," he said to Dan, "but I'm not used to your cold mountain nights." Rapidly he stripped off his clothes, leaving nothing but a brief pair of shorts and a broad belt of a dull metalic red. His arms seemed oddly wrinkled and baggy until Dan realized something was strapped to them.

Greer grimaced slightly as he removed strip after strip of tape from around his arms, loosing a leathery membrane that flapped down below them. Dan remembered the roll of tape in the hotel bathroom and could have laughed. The FBI wouldn't have done much better with that clue!

Then Greer began unstrapping something from one leg. In a moment, a long tail was writhing about, flexing cramped muscles. It reached up, and the broad lozenge-shaped pad at the end deftly opened a compartment in the belt, while one hand dropped in several small instruments.

Dan looked at the creature before him and had a hard time even thinking of it as David Greer. It reached up its arms and, as it flexed them, loose struts in the wings snapped into rigidity.

He looked at Dan and smiled, the smile still oddly human and reassuring. "Well, I guess its time for the reinforcements. Keep a sharp lookout up here, and let us know the moment you spot anything."

Taking a few springy steps to the cliff's edge, he abruptly spread out his arms, for the first time showing the full span of his wings. Dan was hit with primordial dread. The dark, winged creature was something out of nightmare. Involuntarily he stepped back.

Muscles tensing in the moonlight, the creature crouched down. Then with an astonishingly powerful leap, it launched itself into empty space. A few thrusts of the wings sent it climbing up, the tail stretching out behind like a rudder. Then the dark shape leveled out and began soaring slowly down into the silent, moon-washed valley.

Chapter 10

Carla crouched on the hard, gravelly earth. The gnarled pine tree cast spidery moon shadows all around her. Like a frightened hare, her ears pricked for the slightest noise, but there was nothing. A great silence seemed to lie around her, broken now and again by tiny rustlings of night creatures in the dry grass. In the distance, a coyote howled. A lonely, longing sound. Farther away, on the edge of hearing, another seemed to answer.

Ten feet away, a line of poles marched innocently into the night. Nothing interesting to see there. She turned her attention upward. Jagged peaks were silhouetted against the moon-misted sky, their bulk weighing down upon her.

After a time she sighted a black speck floating

above the cliffs. Gradually it descended, coming nearer and nearer until she could make out the animal form and the expanse of dark wings. Instinctively she shrank back under the tree's sparse cover. In a single moment, all her childhood fears were descending upon her.

With only an occasional movement of wings, the figure came lower and lower. A few yards above the surface, the wings scooped several backstrokes while legs and tail thrust downward. With scarcely a sound, it landed beyond the poles.

"David?" she quavered.

"You were expecting someone else?"

She laughed nervously. "I don't know what I was expecting."

Now, with wings hanging inconspicuously at his sides, he seemed, in this light at least, more human. Briskly he walked to one of the poles and squatted down.

"Come closer," he ordered, "a couple of feet on that side. Good. Be ready to jump through when I disconnect the thing."

He examined the base of the pole, grunted with satisfaction and pulled a small instrument from a compartment in his belt. Carla couldn't make it out except that its surface was faceted like a crystal. There was a faint click, and a piece of the silence changed, as though a noise she hadn't really heard had stopped.

"Now!"

She leaped between the poles, half expecting to

be fried. But nothing happened. Another soundless shift, and Greer stood up. "I think I was able to simulate flow continuity. That break shouldn't be detected. But let's not dawdle. There are too many unpredictables in this whole thing."

As they hurried across the great open space, Carla felt like a fly on a white plate. She wanted to run full out, but on this flat ground Greer, with an odd hunched-up gait, was obviously having trouble. Ahead of them the long, narrow shed stretched like a silver wall across the valley.

At last they reached the door marked "Authorized Personnel Only," and Greer touched the lock with the tool Carla had used before.

"You could make a fortune as a burglar with that," she whispered.

"True, but your currency's no good where I come from."

Once inside with the door closed, Carla breathed more easily. The darkness was total, and she switched on the flashlight. Everything looked much as it had before except for the absence of people. Yet now the huge building was filled with a strange sense of waiting, as is a great beast brooded in the darkness. Nervously she shone the beam down the long silver pipes, but still they vanished into darkness well before the far end.

"All that length's really unnecessary," Greer commented. "When the principle's used to power a starship, the whole engine room's only a fraction this size." He walked toward the terminal and studied it. "Still, they'd refine it in time. But let's just postpone that a bit."

He started walking along the length of clustered pipes. His bare feet padded noiselessly over the cold concrete, making Carla's running shoes sound like clumping boots to her ears.

The passed supporting pillars until he finally stopped at the fourth one. "Put your bag down here," he said after examining the structure a moment. "I'll get started."

He rummaged through the bag, pulling out an assortment of tubes, wires and odd devices and piling them near the pillar. Then rolling onto his back, he squirmed under a web of wires and cables until he was up against the base. For several minutes, as Carla held the light, he examined the intricacies above; then taking one of the tools, he severed the ends of several wires and rearranged their connections.

Carla shone the beam at the angles he directed and watched him work. She was both fascinated and horrified, not by the work but by the worker. The light showed the rippling of oddly arranged muscles on arms and chest. The wings, spread in loose, leathery folds at his sides, rasped dryly on the concrete as he shifted positions. He stared in unblinking concentration, the gold flecks in his owl-round eyes catching and reflecting the light in tiny sparks.

"Can you get the light to shine more down here?" he asked. She tried. "No, I guess you can't quite reach it. Here let me have it." His tail coiled up toward her, its terminal pad wrapping around the flashlight. Bringing it down, it held the light at the needed angle.

At first too dumbfounded to react, Carla finally broke into a head-to-toe shiver. Then mentally stomping her foot, she angrily told herself to cut it out. Focus on the positive! Think how useful it would be to have a tail like that—instead of how creepy.

A thought struck her. One thing humanity would clearly have to work on was racism. If people had trouble over skin color and the shape of noses, how would they react to Greer's kind—or to his friends on the station? She was afraid her own reactions were less than commendable.

She checked her watch several times, feeling increasingly nervous as the minutes crept by. At last Greer gave a mewing sigh, and his tail extended the light back to her. She took it gingerly, resisting the temptation to wipe it off on her jeans.

"Well, that does it. The changes won't be seen, and I've set up bypasses so nothing will appear in electronic checks. Now when they run the thing, instead of moving through space, the energy/matter will collapse in on itself. That's one of their theorized possibilities, so they should readily accept it."

He slid out from under and hurriedly repacked the bag, throwing in all the segments of wire and tubing he'd replaced with materials of his own. "This took me longer than it should have. But I'm just a struggling anthropologist, not an engineer. We'd

129

better move. You found nothing about security patrols, but who knows?"

Hastily Carla reshouldered the pack, and they hurried back along the huge shed. She hadn't realized how far into it they'd come. After a tense eternity, they reached the door; Greer opened it and cautiously looked out as Carla switched off the flashlight. The moon was higher in the sky. But otherwise nothing had changed. The world seemed sleepy and unaware.

They slipped out, closing and locking the door behind them. Carla took grateful breaths of the cold night air. Aware suddenly of the temperature, she turned to her companion.

"Are you cold?"

"Very. Flitting around your frigid world without my fur calls for hardship pay. Better call up Dan and tell him we're finished and are on our way back."

Caral did, looking up to the black cliffs as she talked hurriedly with their hidden companion. Then scanning the area once more, they trotted across the yawning open space to the row of poles.

"Will you fly over?" Carla asked.

"Can't risk it. Low as they are, I might not clear the current. On this planet, I really need height to take off. But I can set the break for delayed return—a couple of seconds maybe."

Again he pulled out his faceted tool and tampered with the base of a pole. "Jump through . . . now!"

Carla leaped between two poles, and a split second later Greer followed. "Clear flying now," he said with obvious relief. "Just get to the fence, climb over, and scramble back up there."

Carla looked up doubtfully at the dark, towering mountains. Hardly as easy as he made it sound. But the worse, at least, was over.

Since his companion's astonishing departure from the clifftop, Dan had kept attentive watch. Lying on his stomach at the rock's edge, he'd followed that chillingly beautiful descent with the binoculars. Then he alternated watching his fellows with scanning the buildings and fences.

Everything seemed quiet down below. Once a light switched on in one of the buildings, going off again a few minutes later. Probably a bathroom. The glasses showed him nothing else besides a pair of antelope feeding outside the fence.

Several times he heard coyotes call and remembered Greer's reference to wild animals. Coyotes were supposed to be harmless to people, weren't they? But what about wolves? Or mountain lions? He slipped a hand into his pocket and touched the cold metal of Greer's weapon. Recalling its force he pulled back his hand as if it were burned. Anything that did what this did without using special effects was nothing he wanted to fool with.

When the two disappeared into the long shed, Dan continued his systematic sweeps with the glasses. No threat that he could see. He wished he'd been the one to go down there. Bravado aside, at least he'd be *doing* something. Having to wait alone, on this dark mountain, in the middle of nowhere, wasn't his idea of a fun evening. He smiled. It certainly wasn't what he'd had in mind when he picked up that calculator.

It was hard to believe how much had happened since then. There was no question about it—he had really hated that little guy. Now he liked him. No, more than that: he considered him a friend. And that, as much as anything else, is what kept him clinging to this cold rock on this insane quest.

But wasn't this what he had wanted, he thought wryly? To matter, to make a difference on his own? Certainly if this worked, it would make a difference— a big one. And it wasn't much more bizarre than hopping around with signs on a convention floor. But it was a good deal more dangerous. He tried to imagine Watson and Holmes in this situation, but decided they wouldn't get themselves into anything as off the wall. Now, Indiana Jones, maybe. But fictional companions didn't seem to be help much here. This was all too real.

He jerked with alarm when the walkie-talkie buzzed. "We're through," Carla's voice squawked. "And on our way back."

"Did it work?"

"David said it did. And now I just want out of here fast. Wish you could beam us up."

"Talk to David, that's his department. Be careful."

"Don't worry. Over and out."

He put the walkie-talkie down on the rock ledge and picked up the binoculars. He could see them now, leaving the shadow of the shed. At this distance, Carla's companion didn't look all that inhuman, just eccentric maybe. A little guy in a rain cape.

They reached the poles, stopping for a moment while David did something, then jumped through the invisible barrier. No alarms that he could hear. He felt a surge of relief. In a few hours they'd be back on the road, returning to the real world. The round of rallies and dinners campaigning with his dad had never sounded so good.

He swiveled his glasses away for one more sweep of the valley, then froze. He'd caught a glint of light. Lowering the glasses, he peered in that direction. Bouncing along the road to the complex came a pair of headlights. Already it was very near.

Suddenly bathed in sweat, he looked back to the others. He couldn't find them. No, there they were. Almost to the fence. But the road ran right by there!

He thrust out a hand for the walkie-talkie. His fingers grazed its edge, skidding it over the rock. He lunged for it. Fingers brushed the leather strap as it lurched outward, hurtling into space. His heart froze at the long silence, and then the tiny smashing far below.

Emptiness flowed into panic. He looked up, gripping the glasses fiercely. The car was nearer. His friends had slowed down. They'd never get over the fence in time! What could he do? It was too far to yell or jump up and down. If only they'd see the lights!

"Hold up," Greer called wearily as Carla jogged on ahead. "I've had it with running. Just not built for it."

Reluctantly she slowed. "Don't you have any big open spaces at home?"

"Hardly any. It's a hot dry place, mostly mountains and valleys—steep ones. We build our cities in cliffs. To get places, our ancestors flew or climbed—never ran."

"Well, what about—"

"Wait, do you hear something?"

They paused. The night silence was underlain by a faint rumbling.

"A car!" she said.

"Yes. But where? It couldn't be close, or Dan would have warned us. But let's get moving!"

They sprinted toward the fence. Carla reached it first and was scrambling awkwardly up when David sprang to the top and clinging with toes and tail, reached down to help her.

She vaulted over and down, feet jarring heavily on the rocky ground. Greer landed lightly beside her. They'd just started across the road, when a pickup truck rose out of a dip and caught them squarely in its headlights. Like deer, they froze for a second, then bolted across the road.

"Hey you!" a voice called from the truck. "Stop!"

The two saboteurs fled into the scrub, but there was little cover. The truck's engine roared in protest as the driver slammed down the accelerator and set off cross country after them.

"Stop! This is a restricted area. Stop, or we'll shoot!"

The dark cliffs loomed ahead, still too distant for Carla as she leaped wildly over rocks and sage. A shot rang out. Then another. Real gunfire! At her!

Indignant and terrified, she spun around. Greer had dropped slightly behind, but the ground was rockier now and the truck had slowed.

She pounded on. The cliffs were closer. The truck farther behind. Suddenly she stumbled over a fallen log. At the same instant, the truck jogged over a rise and swept them with its headlights.

Another shot. With a strangled cry, Greer crumpled to the ground. For an instant, Carla froze. Then she flung herself back over the log. Bending low, she scrambled back to find Greer just staggering to his feet.

"You're shot!"

"Not badly. Got to head for that gap in the cliffs."

They veered to the right, Greer limping. Twice he grabbed at Carla for support. The ground was boulder-strewn now. Far behind them the truck had stopped. Shouting at them, two men got out of the cab and followed.

After a lung-bursting eternity, they stumbled

into the dark ravine Greer had pointed out. No moonlight fell into the narrow canyon, but to Carla's dismay she saw that it ended almost at once in a vertical stone wall.

"We're trapped!" she sobbed breathlessly

"No, saved." Leaning against the cold stone, Greer flicked at his belt, drawing out the end of a thin cord. He plucked at a section, widening it into a broad band that he quickly wrapped around Carla's waist.

"You'll have to help me as much as you can," he said. Then suddenly he leaped onto the cliff face, and using hands, toes and tail, he scrambled up. Attached by the cord, Carla was jerked after him.

Desperately, she searched for foot- and handholds, anything to take some of her weight off him. She clamped her mind onto that search, not daring to think of the emptiness below her.

Like a lizard he climbed up and up, until Carla suddenly found herself clinging to a narrow ledge with Greer, wheezing for breath, crouched close beside her. His naked thigh, pressing against hers, oozed a dark warm liquid.

"You're bleeding!"

"Hush," he whispered. "They're coming."

Seconds later the rasp of boots on rock rose from the mouth of the gorge. "They went in here," a voice said. Footsteps. A flashlight played over the tiny canyon floor and part way up the walls. Carla pressed her face into the cold stone, willing herself to look like granite.

"It's a dead end. They couldn't have gone this way."

"But I saw them duck in here."

"Then they must've ducked out again. Come on. They couldn't have gone far. We hit one of them."

The voices and footsteps moved away. Carla let out her breath, and realized Greer was shivering. "Can you make it farther?" Her apprehension was both for him and herself. The sense of height hit her. Without him she'd be like a panicky kitten trapped on a branch.

"Have to. They may be back." Wedging himself into a crack in the rock, he worked his way upward with Carla half dragging and half climbing behind.

The crack widened. He sprang to a projecting ledge, missed and slithered down. Carla squealed in terror as she dropped several feet then stopped with a jerk. He tried again. For an awful moment, she was yanked free of her hold and swung through space to smash against another rock face. Tearing her nails, she clutched at the rough surface, clinging almost by sheer will.

The upward tug began again. Impossibly she found shallow holds. The climb seemed endless. In patches the rock surface was smeared with sticky liquid. She wanted to cry—for him, for herself, for the world. Instead she climbed.

At last the tug on the cord slackened. With bloody hands, she pulled herself up over a ledge. Shaking with fear and exhaustion, she looked around. They were on the clifftop. A few feet from her, Greer was slumped against a rock sobbing for breath. Getting dizzily to her feet, she staggered toward him.

"Got to get to the cave," he gasped.

"Here, put your arm around me." Kneeling beside him, she helped him throw a frail arm over her shoulders. She shuddered as the leathery wing slithered across her back. Firmly she suppressed her rising horror. This was a friend who'd struggled to save her. He needed her help.

Together, they took several faltering steps. Suddently his legs collapsed under him. Groaning he sagged to the ground in a heap.

Carla knelt down grabbing his hand. "Come on. We'll make it."

Feebly his hand squeezed hers. "Yes," he whispered. "I've come to love your world. But don't want . . . to die here."

Chapter 11

Panic threatened to drown him. From his helpless distance, Dan watched the truck and the fleeing figures coming closer and closer together. They were up and over the fence—and right into the headlights!

He closed his eyes, stifling the scream in his mind. If he was to help his friends, he'd have to stay calm. Opening his eyes, he forced himself to watch with cold detachment. They were running through the scrub beyond the road. The truck stopped, then jolted after. He must get closer, get above them on the cliff. He didn't know how, but if he were nearer, maybe he could help.

Running and jumping over shelves of rock, he kept his flashlight switched off. The moonlight was enough and shouldn't give him away to watchers below. The sound of gunfire jolted him, but he kept his mind on the need to hurry, to get nearer.

Another shot. He couldn't stand it. Stopping, he trained the glasses on the scene below. Oh, God, one of them was down! Shot? Then they were up, moving again. The truck had slowed.

The fugitives veered in his direction, and he lost them under the lip of the cliff. He kept working down and over to where he had seen them last. Long minutes passed. Half an hour, maybe more. He tried to be silent and careful and fast, and to somehow get to the right place—wherever that was.

Suddenly he knew he'd found it. On a rock clifftop one, no, two figures crouched. He scrambled over to them.

Carla looked up. "Thank God!"

"David?" he asked.

"He's shot, in the leg. And he practically dragged me up here. Said to get him to the cave. I think he needs something there."

Dan switched on his light and beamed it on the crumpled figure. The skin, which earlier had seemed human enough, was a pale gray. And his leg . . . They both gasped as they saw it in the light. A huge chunk of his thigh had been blown away. The ragged edges of the wound oozed with a thick black liquid. His face was drawn, his eyes closed as he breathed in shallow gasps.

"Come on," Dan said. "We'll carry him. He's awfully light."

He knelt down, slipping one arm under the legs, the other under the winged shoulders. He stood up, scarcely staggering, and headed up the slope. A memory struck him. He'd carried his dog once, like this, when it had been hit by a car. Bleeding and dying. The dog had been heavier. Please God, don't let him die. He's your creature, too.

Climbing steadily, he tried to retrace his route, surprised at how clear it was in his mind. When he grew tired, Carla took over. The only sound from their limp burden was rasping breathing and an occasional moan if they stumbled and jarred him.

The climb seemed endless, but finally the bare granite dome stretched before them in the moonlight. Dan hurried across it to the cave. Gently he lowered Greer to the cold stone floor.

Greer groaned and opened his eyes. The swimming flecks reflected the light Carla had switched on. "The other pack," he said weakly. "Was a fool to leave it out . . . worried about weight."

Carla rushed to the mouth of the cave and hauled back the pack they had left behind. Feebly Greer waved at it. "Inside, . . . a small blue tube. Get it."

She fumbled inside, pulling out everything but the food. Among a handful of suspiciously alien items was a three-inch-long blue tube. She handed it to Greer. Grimacing with pain, he struggled to sit up. Hastily Dan moved to help him, letting him lean on a supporting arm.

Carla shone the light on the gaping hole in his

leg. Greer's hand shook as he twisted one end of the tube and lowered it. A pearly mist swirled forth, filling the wound and quickly solidifying.

In moments, the cavity was gone. Gently Greer smoothed his fingers over the slick gray surface. Dan, who'd been watching in amazement, said, "What's that, instant flesh?"

Greer shook his head. The tightness and pain had already left his voice. "No, a medicinal filler. It'll start generating new blood and tissue. Our bones and flesh are very porous—for lightness. But as a result we're vulnerable to projectiles. A big one can shatter us."

He sagged back against Dan's arm. "I've got to rest. Sorry . . . can't help it." He sounded groggy now. There must be a strong pain killer in that stuff, Dan thought as he lowered him down again. Already Greer's eyes were closed, and he curled up like a cat, draping one wing around himself.

They picked up his clothes from beside the pack and spread them over him. Then taking the pack with them, they tiptoed outside, though they doubted anything, short of a bomb, could wake him.

The two sat down on the moon-whitened rock. Rummaging through the pack, Carla pulled out a couple of candy bars and handed one to Dan. Donning extra jackets, they huddled together against a cold that came from more than the mountain night. They were shaken and afraid.

Eating hungrily, they exchanged experiences.

Carla described her descent, the time in the shed and that awful climb. Dan confessed about the walkie-talkie and his own panicky frustration.

Carla shrugged it off. "That's the breaks. They might have seen us anyway. And if we'd been caught actually inside the fence, it would have been worse."

"What do you think they'll do now?"

"Nothing probably 'til morning. David's fiddling with those poles seemed to have worked, so they oughtn't to guess how far we got. But they're pretty edgy with that test coming up. Mom said they were aiming to do it in just thirteen days."

Dan put an arm around Carla's shoulder, not a romantic move, but a need for human companionship. They looked out at the sleeping valley, the westering moon and the cold, distant stars.

"I hope he'll be all right," Carla whispered. "To be hurt, maybe die, so far from home . . ." She shuddered, moving closer.

"I know. He's . . . he's really a good person, when you get to know him. It must have been hard for him, all these years. I guess he asked for it, but we all did treat him terribly." Dan was silent awhile, then continued. "To be honest, I almost wish we hadn't had to do this. I mean, it'd be great getting to know his people—maybe even some of those others, weird as they look. Sounds like it's teeming with them out there." He gestured at the sparkling sky.

"But we're not ready for them, you known," Carla said. Pictures ran through her mind like a newscast. Hatred and riots, wars and the willingness to let people starve and suffer.

"I know. But it is a future to look forward to—for someone anyway."

The excitement and nervous energy of the night had seeped away, and they were both suddenly very tired. Oblivious to the cold and the hardness of the rock, they lay back and were soon deeply asleep.

Dan awoke, stiff and cold. The moon hung much closer to the western horizon. Around him, the darkness rippled with new bird calls. The sky was still black in the east, but clearly dawn was not far off.

Suddenly, there was a rustling behind them and a few unintelligible words. Dan spun around, his light flashing toward the cave. Greer was sitting up, staring intently into the sky beyond them.

"They're coming!"

"Who?"

"Helicopters. No. Only one, I think."

"I don't hear anything," Carla said, awake now. Then she stopped. Very faintly a clucking sound floated through the night.

"In here, out of sight!" Greer said staggering to his feet. The young people bolted for the cave.

"Should you be standing?" Carla asked anxiously as Greer pulled on his clothes.

"Not really. But it's nearly healed. Could've used a few more hours, though."

The steady whir of the helicopter was closer. Leaning cautiously out the entrance, Dan saw it and quickly pulled back. A cluster of hovering lights was working its way along the edge of the cliff, scouring it up and down with a brilliant searchlight.

"They're searching for us all right," Carla said. "They must be jumpier than I thought."

"There're several military bases in the area," Greer commented. "They probably called one for help. Wainwright must have given the military standing orders to help this project any way they could—and at any hour, it seems."

The machine's noise and lights came relentlessly nearer. "Shouldn't we make a break for it?" Dan asked.

"No," Greer replied. "They might see us. We don't know the sort of detection equipment they have, but the cave's overhang should shield us from sight and probably from heat sensors."

Like a menacing bird of prey, the copter moved closer, the questing light exposing every rock and weed as it passed. Carla shivered. "If there's one thing I hate, it's things coming at me out of the sky." Quickly she glanced at Greer. "Sorry. Nothing personal."

"That's okay. We all have our phobias. I hate water. We haven't much at home, and a lot of it unnerves me."

The noise grew, drowning out their words, even

their thoughts. It seemed the air was chopped noisily to pieces and hurled down around them. The searchlight, aimed now on the cliff below them, gradually worked its way up to sweep over the broad rock ledge. The blinding light lay bare every inch of granite, and something more as well—an incongruous splash of blue.

"The other pack!" Carla exclaimed.

It had not gone unnoticed by those above. The whirring and searchlight hung motionless above them, while the small blue pack remained mercilessly exposed.

After a frozen moment, Dan shouted, "We've got to get out of here!" But Greer was already stuffing everything loose into the remaining pack.

"Let's go!" he yelled over the roar. Flattening himself against the rock, he slipped out. The projecting rock overhang barely hid them and the cave from view and kept the sea of blinding light a few feet off.

Three terrified shadows, they flitted along under the jutting rock until a narrow brush-filled ravine led them into welcome darkness away from the cliff's edge. Behind them the thunderous noise slowly lowered. Obviously the pack was a clue the searchers had every intention of retrieving.

Fear, like a pursuing beast, kept them moving at a speed the two humans would have thought impossible. Greer's night vision kept them to their route. But while he had led before, he now had difficulty keeping up. His limp was pronounced.

At last, shaking and out of breath, they stumbled to a halt among a grove of spindly pines. Greer sank down at the base of a tree and rubbed his leg.

"Are you okay?" Carla asked with concern.

"Yes. But worried. What was in that pack?"

"Just food, wasn't it?" Carla said after a moment.

"And one canteen," Dan added.

"Good," Greer said. "Then there's nothing incriminating. Nothing to link us to that complex."

"But there is the location," Dan pointed out. "The perfect spot to spy on those buildings."

"It could be coincidence," Greer said.

Carla shook her head. "Then why did we run when they caught us down there?"

"Just two inquisitive campers afraid to get entangled with authorities?" Greer suggested. "And there's no way to know when the pack was left, nor that we came back up here, particularly not up that sheer cliff."

"What about the blood?" Carla said. "It's all over some of those rocks."

Greer snorted. "I doubt they'd recognize it as blood. Motor oil maybe." Grabbing on to the tree trunk, he hauled himself to his feet. "But let's get going. Come morning there's sure to be a search.

The fainter stars were already fading from the sky as a pearly gray spread from the east. Over the far mountain, the morning star hung alone, like a glistening teardrop. Dry leaves of sage and manzanita rustled in a chill predawn breeze.

The three plunged on through gradually increasing light. Dan and Carla found it a relief to see obstacles clearly rather than feel them with bruised legs and hands. The eastern sky blushed pink until an orange chink appeared over the far peaks and swelled into a glowing sun.

As the first rays touched them with a breath of warmth, Greer stopped to put on his dark glasses. Dan and Carla looked at each other, sharing a shocked realization. They'd gotten used to the strangeness of his eyes.

The morning passed slowly, the temperature rising from welcome warmth, through comfort, to baking heat. They were tired, hungry and increasingly thirsty. Carefully they shared out the warm water in the two remaining canteens. Several hours after dawn they saw a distant helicopter coasting over the side of the mountains they'd left. Minutes later it was joined by two others, and the formation disappeared from view.

It was midmorning when they reached the rock of Indian petroglyphs. Gratefully they collapsed under its familiar shelter. They shared the last drops in one canteen and watched the northern sky where a mosquito-sized helicopter crossed and recrossed in an orderly search pattern.

"They really pushed the panic button, didn't they?" Dan said. "I wonder if there're ground troops, too."

148

Greer who'd been slumped against a rock, sat up at this. "I hope not. But have you two got your IDs ready, the ones I gave you?"

They both nodded, patting pockets.

"Good. Hope we won't need them. But they're state-of-the-art."

A whirring swooped down on them from the west. They cringed back under their rock as another helicopter swung over and flew off to the north.

Carla shivered. "This is like the movies. Only I'd rather be on the other side eating popcorn."

When the blue dome of sky was clear of all but circling hawks, they set off again. Heat beat down at them from the sun and bounced back from the bare rock.

They came to a spot Dan remembered from their trek out. The trail Greer followed was barely visible. And here it crossed a steep slope that clearly served as a regular route for landslides. The surface, strewn with rock chips and loose gravel, was very slippery. Dan fought the temptation to get down on hands and knees and crawl across.

Greer, surefooted as ever, led the way. Close behind him, Carla tried to move and think like a mountain goat. Dan hung back, then forced himself to step out on the scree, feeling carefully with each footstep. Gradually he got into the rhythm of it and moved faster.

He was nearly across when suddenly a flat rock

slid beneath his foot. Both legs shot out from under him, and he fell heavily on one side.

Instantly, he was rocketing down the steep slope. Flailing arms and legs, he tried desperately to grab something stable. But the whole hillside seemed to be moving with him.

Glancing jerkily between his feet, he saw with horror that he was shooting toward a rocky ledge. He hit it with a jolt and abruptly arched through the air. Much sooner than he feared, he came to earth, smashing into a clump of sagebrush. He sprawled there, stunned and shaking, while a rain of loose rock and gravel clattered around him.

Expecting the worst, he inventoried his body. His hands were scraped and bloody, and every inch of him hurt. But everything did seem to move. He could scarcely believe he hadn't broken anything. He opened his mouth to call to the others, when he heard another voice. A man's voice, and it wasn't Greer's.

"Halt! Who's there?"

Dan froze. Through the tangle of sage, he glimpsed movement. Something in olive drab. A soldier! They *had* sent in ground troops.

"Whoever's there, stay where you are! I'm armed." The soldier was moving nearer, but Dan realized he hadn't been seen yet.

He would be in a moment though, and it would be over. Everything would be over. If only he could just disappear from here. Beam me up, Scotty, he thought desperately. But there was no *Star Trek* technology here. He was on his own.

No, the thought hit him, not entirely. No transporters, but maybe a phaser. He slid a hand into his pocket and pulled out the cold metal disk. But that was as far as he got. He couldn't zap that soldier.

Still . . . Trying not to move the crackling sage, he looked around. He had to try something. The soldier was some twenty feet below him and to the right. If he thought this whole thing was just another natural landslide and not a clumsy spy . . .

Dan aimed the front of the disk just behind a basketball-sized rock on the slope between him and the soldier. Holding his breath, he pressed the knob. The air quivered in a nearly invisible ribbon. The spot of ground jerked into dust. Immediately, the rock shivered and began rolling down the slope, bringing more and more small rocks with it.

The soldier yelped and jumped clear of the new landslide. When the noise and dust finally settled, he muttered something and turned back, taking a lower and safer route in his search.

For minutes, Dan lay motionless in the bush, miserably uncomfortable but afraid to make the slightest move. Sharp twigs jabbed him everywhere, and he was submerged in the pungent smell of dust and broken sage. Then came a faint rattle of stones from above and Greer's hushed voice.

"He's gone now, heading northwest." With an

agile leap he landed on the ledge beside the clump of sage. "That was good thinking, Dan. Saved the day for us. Are you hurt?"

"Yes. But not enough for casts and slings—I think."

With Greer's help, he scrambled out of the bush. After finding that his legs still supported him, they hurried with heightened caution to the tumbled boulders where Carla waited.

Her face lit up when she saw Dan in one piece. She jumped up and hugged him. "I thought we were on our way to Sing Sing until you did that trick with the rock. A special effects genius!"

He blushed under his layer of dust. "It's just the fancy technology." He pulled the disk from his pocket and extended it to Greer. "Here. Thanks for trusting me with it."

"Keep it. A souvenir of how you saved the world. Let's go. The sooner we're out of here the better. This whole thing is sorely trying my commitment to anthropology."

They hurried on their way, constantly looking about them, jumping at every sound. But they saw no more soldiers and caught only one glimpse of a helicopter as it crossed the mountains way to their south.

It was midafternoon when Greer called a halt and sank wearily onto a rock outcrop. "The van's just around the corner, but I'm putting on these wretched shoes first." He started unlacing the tennis shoes from his belt. Then grinning, he looked up at them. "You know, the three of us really are a sight. We look like we've been wandering in the wilderness for months."

Dan and Carla looked at each other and laughed. Their clothes were torn and their arms and faces were covered with scrapes and bruises; Carla's from her climb and Dan's from his fall. Carla's black lustrous hair was whitened with dust. And Dan's perpetually messy mop was studded with burrs and sage twigs.

"Indiana Jones and the girl never look like this," Dan observed as they both ran fingers through their hair.

"The magic of Hollywood," Greer said. "You two go on down to the van and get yourselves some water while I put on these instruments of torture. Then it's home free."

They didn't need urging. Rounding a boulder, the two saw the van below them, waiting as if they had left it for a picnic a few hours earlier. The cool afternoon shadows of the pines filled the ravine with a timeless calm.

Carla sobbed with joy. "I bet your dad doesn't want the White House as much as I wanted this place."

Dan could only nod.

Eagerly they trotted down the slope, thinking of long wet drinks from the jug in the back of the van. Suddenly they skidded to a halt. A stony-faced young soldier stepped out from behind the van.

"Is this your vehicle?" he demanded.

For a moment they only stared at him, feeling their hopes topple like a tower of blocks.

"Yes," Dan answered finally.

"Well, not really ours," Carla elaborated. "It's the professor's. Professor Cavendish's."

Looking quickly up the ravine she yelled, "Oh Professor, there's a gentleman here in a uniform to see you."

The noise startled a crow, which rose squawking from the pines. For a moment nothing else happened. Then a figure with dark glasses and a slight limp appeared from around a boulder and walked sedately toward them.

Carla turned back to the soldier. "We've been looking for Indian petroglyphs, you see. Professor Cavendish is a world-famous expert in the field."

"And we found some, too!" Dan added brightly. "Some that weren't even recorded. Let me show you the guide." Slipping the pack from his back, he began rummaging through it while Carla carried on.

"And we found artifacts, too! This one's the best." She pulled from her pocket the arrowhead she'd found at the complex.

The soldier had tried to remain professionally aloof, but he clearly had a weakness for arrowheads. He took it and turned it over in his hands. "Nice one." He hastily handed it back as the man approached.

"Well, young man, am I getting a ticket for parking here?" He followed with a chirping laugh.

"Your van was spotted from the air, and we were sent to investigate. May I see your identification, please?"

"Identification? Certainly, certainly." He dug into a pocket in his jeans and, pulling out a worn leather wallet, handed it to the soldier.

The other opened it and looked through all the contents. Dr. Stanley J. Cavendish. Professor of Anthropology at the Univesrity of Southern Oregon. Amoco credit card, Ashland Public Library Card, Blue Cross, Drivers license expiring next year, Mastercharge, voter registration card, membership in the Jackson County Historical Society, sixty-two dollars in cash, several stamps, scraps of paper with phone numbers and grocery lists.

The soldier closed the wallet. Handing it back, he looked at the other two. Greer volunteered, "These are students of mine, Carla Brewster and Dan McIntosh. They're part of an archaeological summer school. Do you need to see their IDs too?" he asked with mild surprise.

Dan and Carla looked up innocently from their guide book and began fumbling in their pockets.

"No," the young man said turning back to the professor. "I need to know how long you've been here, where you've gone, and if you've seen anyone else in these mountains."

"Well, we got here night before last, and spent the day looking for sites just south of here. I can show you on the map. Here . . . this area with the dots.

Then we came back to the van for the night and today we concentrated more in this other area. Found a new site too, not on the maps. But I confess, our eyes were mostly for rocks, not people. Though there were some helicopters about today. And come to think of it, when we were eating lunch, we did see someone on another ridge. Dan here thought it looked like a soldier. Are there some escaped prisoners about, or something?"

"Not that meet your description. Thank you for your time, Professor. Sorry to have bothered you."

"Oh, no bother," he said as the other turned away. "Hope everything works out." The young man walked down the slope to the jeep, which had been concealed behind the pines. Another soldier waited at the wheel.

Ten minutes after the jeep had disappeared, the van was loaded and heading off in the opposite direction, its dust plume a hasty scribble in the clear western sky.

"Well," Dan said when they'd hit a semblance of road and were not jolting too much to talk, "that was a fun-filled five days."

Carla laughed. "What I did on my summer vacation, a ready-made essay."

"And now, thankfully, back to the real world," Greer said. "Legitimate Indian studies for you, Carla, and the campaign trail for us."

Dan thought how ordinary and safe all that would seem now. With it he realized something else, and the thought surprised him. He no longer viewed it all with such dissatisfaction. He had done his own thing, something unquestionably important. Maybe the world would never know, but he would. And that was enough for now.

After a while he turned to the driver. "David, will you stay with us until the election?"

"Certainly. The race isn't won yet, just the worst pitfall avoided."

"And after that, what are your plans?"

"Well, if your dad doesn't win, I'll probably be asked to stay on as part of the protectorate. But it's not something I want. It's terribly unprofessional for an anthropologist, but I've grown too fond of this culture to willingly to preside over its death.

"But if he wins, I'm hoping your dad will make me Presidential Science Advisor. Then I can work to set research developments on the right track—or the wrong one, depending on your point of view."

Carla was tracing and retracing a finger over the design on her bracelet. "No, David, it *is* the right one if it gives us a chance to get our act together."

He smiled at them. "I hope it will. You two work on that end."

For a while they jounced along in silence, except for the steady rumble of the van. A lean, long-eared jackrabbit sat on its haunches, watching their approach, then bounded off over the scrubland.

Greer continued, a happy lilt in his now familiarly accented voice. "Then as soon as I possibly can, I'm going home. I've been doing some serious thinking career-wise. Maybe I'll get out of anthropology altogether and into some quiet, unstressful field—like politics maybe."